Alan Smith lives and works i first novel.

big
soft
lads

ALAN SMITH

review

First published in this edition in 1997
by HEADLINE BOOK PUBLISHING

A REVIEW paperback

10 9 8 7 6 5 4 3 2 1

ISBN 0 7472 5676 4

Typeset by
Letterpart Limited, Reigate, Surrey
Printed and bound in Great Britain by
Clays Ltd, St Ives plc.

HEADLINE BOOK PUBLISHING
A division of Hodder Headline PLC
338 Euston Road
London NW1 3BH

big soft
lads

PROLOGUE

At the end of his first term in York, just before Christmas, Les had been out on his own. He met Charles Wilson and they fell in love. There was nothing to be done, no way of knowing.

Les had been sitting in a pub on King's Staithe watching the darts match. If he hadn't been drunk he wouldn't have waited. A man in a tight black tee-shirt looked over at Les, staring.

'Getting a bit of hard eye,' said Les, mumbling, then laughing. Black tee-shirt turned away, waited for his friend to pull his darts from the board. He threw: triple one, five and off the board. He looked at Les. Les waved at him, smiled. Black tee-shirt picked up a bottle, two quick steps and hit Les over the top of the head with it. Les clutched his head and fell over the table. The young man pulled his darts, picked up his coat and walked towards the door. His friend followed him.

'Fucking student,' he said.

Les looked at his hands. They were bloody. The two men were standing at the door. A big man with a red face was standing at the top of the steps which led out of the pub down to the quayside. He was poking black tee-shirt with his blunt finger, not letting him past. Les got up.

1

Alan Smith

'Hey,' he shouted. Black tee-shirt turned round. 'Look at this.' Les showed his bloody head and hands to the bouncer. He was close now. Black tee-shirt squared up to him. Les ignored him. 'Blood,' he said, shocked, to the bouncer and kicked black tee-shirt in the balls. He fell into the bouncer and they both went down the steps.

Then Les was on the carpet. Someone was kicking him, trying to stamp on him, as he rolled over, banging into tables, trying to climb up people's legs. He got up, sat on someone. A blond-haired boy with a thin, broken nose was standing over black tee-shirt's friend, hit him once, twice with a wooden chair. Les grabbed the boy by his coat lapel and ran him down the stairs, past the bouncer and black tee-shirt, on to Lendal Bridge and away.

They had sat in the hospital together. Les held a wad of tissue on the top of his head. His hair was stiff with blood.

'Bit of a mess, that shirt.' The blond boy had smiled as he said it.

'Ribs I'm worried about,' Les told him. 'Bit good with that chair you were. Preferred weapon is it?'

'Ah well,' said the blond boy, 'no good pausing for thought in that sort of situation.'

'Leslie Holland,' a woman's voice. They both looked down the corridor.

'That's you, is it?'

'Yes,' said Les.

'Charles Wilson,' said the blond boy and held out his hand. Les shook it.

'Do you always talk like a judge?' Les asked him.

A tall impatient young woman, a nurse, was staring at them, tapping a pen on a plastic clipboard. Les stood up,

2

startled. Nausea hit him in the face and he fell backwards on to Charles.

Les was conscious again. He was on his back, his head pulsing.

'Who's he, then?' the nurse asked. She looked up from taping his ribs.

'Dunno,' said Les.

'You covered him nicely in sick,' she told him.

'Still there, is he?'

'Made him wait. If there's nobody to take you away we'll have to keep you in.' She pulled back the screen of curtains and Les saw Charles sitting across the room.

'You clumsy prick,' said Charles. 'Just look. It stinks.'

'I'm your responsibility,' Les told him. 'She says so,' pointing at the nurse.

'That's right,' she said, 'and you can go now. Go on, push off.' She scowled and walked out of the room.

CHAPTER ONE

The girl in the silver dress did her best with Les Holland, but whenever she got him to his feet he fell down again.

'Bugger you,' she said and kicked him in the ribs.

'No, no,' said Les and looked up at her from where he was lying on the lawn. He rolled over on to his back and spread his arms wide. The rain fell on to his face and he screwed up his face and opened his mouth.

'Come on, come inside,' she told him, angry, pleading.

'All wet now. Doesn't matter.' He looked up at her. Her hair was plastered round her face like a head scarf, her dress was soaked and clung to her.

'Give us a kiss,' he said.

'Inside,' she insisted.

'Promise?'

'Anything,' she shouted at him.

He rolled over and started to crawl on his hands and knees towards the house. He went in a straight line; across the lawn, into the fish pond, across a flower bed and on to the patio. He sat down in front of the French windows.

'Can't reach the knob,' he said. She ran up the steps and stood over him. He was covered in slime and mud. She looked inside. There was a smoky blue light, a dozen or so people were sitting or lying on the furniture and floor. They would never make it across the room. She grabbed his arm and pulled him up and across the patio until, five or six yards on, she had him by the door to the kitchen. He sat on the floor again when she let go of him to open the door.

'Oh, you can't go in like that,' she wailed at him.

'Very happy here,' he said with affected dignity. He sat back against the wall and wiped the rain from his face, leaving muddy smudges around his eyes. 'Go and get us a drink.'

'Right, fine.' She went into the kitchen and in a few moments reappeared with a bottle of beer. 'Stay like that,' she said and went back inside. He sat drinking the beer, began to feel cold, but a little clearer. She came back carrying a large orange bucket.

'Put your legs out straight, Les.'

'Ah no, Deborah. Don't.'

'It's hot water. You'll like it, honest.' He put his legs out straight, covered the neck of his beer bottle with one hand and screwed up his eyes. She poured the water in a steady stream over his head and shoulders and down each arm. He tried to get up but she pushed him down. 'Stay,' she said. She came back with another bucketful and rinsed off his legs.

He sat still for a minute and then said, 'Can you take me home?'

'Take your clothes off,' she said.

'Can I stay?' he asked. She shrugged. He started to undress.

All day there had been sunshine but, even in summer, York was suddenly miserable in the rain. There were no lights in the houses and the rain made the blackness of the night close and cold.

Charles stood for a few moments, waiting for his breathing to slow. The rain fell, spitefully. He ran off up the hill, towards Micklegate Bar, past the big, flat-fronted houses, past the terrace of shops. He let himself in through the door at the side of the newsagents, slammed it shut and went up the stairs.

The light was on in the kitchen. Dishes were stacked on the draining board. There was new, dirty lino on the floor, four wooden chairs and a faded dining table. He went to his room and brought back a bottle of dark rum, poured a glass half full and added some hot water from the kettle.

He emptied his coat pockets and put on to the table three small, silver boxes and an envelope. He took some five and ten pound notes from the envelope and began to count. There was a hundred and fifty pounds. He took the boxes and the money into his room, put them into the drawer of his desk, went back for the bottle and his glass. He sat on the edge of his bed, towelling his hair and taking sips of the drink.

Outside in the street it was raining steadily. A taxi stopped outside the newsagents. A girl, tall, with long, blonde hair, stood in the rain fumbling to pay the driver. As the taxi drove off she turned and pressed the bell on the door of the flat. She was wearing a white jacket, blue jeans, high-heeled boots. The white jacket was turning dark with the rain, her hair was flat against her head. She kept her finger on the bell. The window above her opened.

'Catch,' he called down to her. The keys bounced on the pavement. Her hands were wet and cold on the metal as she opened the door. She went up the bare, wooden stairs and found him on the bed drinking rum.

'Well, what happened?' she asked.

'I fancied a walk. Then I got wet so I came home. You're all wet too,' he added.

She took off her coat and spread it over the back of his armchair, crossed the room, picked up his towel from the bed and rubbed her hair.

'Anybody miss me?' he asked.

'Only me.'

'You know what I mean. Did anybody mention that I'd gone?'

'Les did and somebody else, that girl he was with, said she'd seen you putting on your coat in the hall.'

'Which one's that? The one in the silver dress?' He got up from the bed before she could answer. 'I'll get you a glass,' he said.

When he came back she was brushing her hair. She took the glass of rum from him and asked, 'Why did you make me go there if you don't like it?'

'Who says I don't like it? Barney's got a nice house there. He fills us all up with drink. What's to dislike? Anyway everybody else was going. You wanted to.'

'Don't leave me there, that's all.'

'I was going to phone. Just now when you came in. I was going to tell you to get a cab and come here and I'd throw the keys down for you.' He lay back on the bed, drinking rum, watching her as she stood brushing her hair. 'Why did you come here?' he asked.

'Charlie,' she said softly, uncertain.

'Take your clothes off,' he said. She looked at his quiet face.

'Can I stay?' she asked. He shrugged. She started to undress.

CHAPTER TWO

'What happened to you?' asked Charles Wilson.

'Don't ask, Chas, don't ask.' Les Holland sat hunched at the kitchen table. 'I'm ever so ill.'

'Yes, you look it.'

'I'm glad you think it's a good thing.' He looked and saw Charles's suit. 'Where've you been?'

'Leeds.'

'Course you have,' he said sarcastically. Then, with mock patience, 'Now, tell me why.'

'I've been selling Barney's snuff boxes.'

'And you left me there?'

'Best place for you.'

'Anyway, shut up for now.' He pointed to the kitchen door. 'In my room.'

'Silver dress?'

'Spot on.'

Charles sat down at the table. 'You look really awful,' he said. 'Have you taken anything?' He looked at Les. 'You know that you smell, don't you? What have you been doing?'

'No, I've not taken anything. Deborah's told me that I'm smelly. And, apparently, I'm smelly because I've been in Barney's fish pond. Okay?'

'That's her name, is it?'

'Give her a shout.'

When Deborah came into the kitchen Charles said, 'Where's your nice dress?'

'I've only just got here. I've been home.' She was wearing black trousers and a red tee-shirt that had printed on it a black clenched fist.

'If you cook him something,' said Charles, 'I'll run him a bath.'

'You cook,' she said and went to the bathroom.

'What's the matter with her?'

'Don't ask,' said Les. Deborah stood in the doorway.

'What do I do with the clothes?' she asked.

'They're in the bath,' Les explained to Charles. 'Throw them away, I reckon. There are some bin bags under the sink.' She banged around the kitchen and flounced off back to the bathroom with the black, plastic bag.

'What's her problem?' said Charles.

'Stage one proprietorship,' said Les cheerfully. 'When you get mad with someone you simultaneously assert that you have the right to get mad with them. She is a woman with rights, drawable on me.'

'What are you going to do?'

'Exploit her a bit and then give her the elbow.'

'Jolly good. Might I exploit her a bit as well?'

'What are you cooking for me?'

'Soup, tomato soup. Ready in ten minutes. Now go and get washed.'

From the doorway Deborah said, 'There was money in your pockets.' She came into the room and put some five pound notes on the table.

'Oh good; give them a rinse for me while I have a soak.'

10

'How much is there?' said Charles.

'Thirty-five pounds,' said Deborah. He came away from stirring the saucepan and picked up the notes.

'They do pong a bit.' He took them to the sink and rinsed each one carefully under the tap and spread them on the draining board. 'My name's Charles,' he said.

She was taken aback. 'I know,' she said uncertainly.

'What do you do,' he asked her, 'a student?'

'Yes. Biology.'

'You cut things up, that sort of thing? Pin things out and pick over their guts?'

'If they've got any.'

'That's right.' He stirred at the red, glutinous soup. 'Want a drink? There should be some wine in the fridge.' She looked in the fridge and held up a bottle.

'This?' she asked. 'Where's the corkscrew?'

'It should be in the drawer, there in the table. Glasses are in the sink.' He held out his hand for the bottle, but she ignored him and pulled the cork herself.

'You want to get one with levers, too much of a fight that one.' She rattled around the sink and found two glasses. 'You're not short of a few bob, you two. It's like Aladdin's cave in Les's room.'

'You think so?'

'What does his father do?'

'He's got a little shop in Northampton. So Les gets a full grant you see.'

'I'll say.'

'Works all summer. Christmas and birthday presents. Mounts up you know.' He took a glass of wine from her, drank a sip of it and went back to the saucepan. 'What about you, your father?'

11

'He works for the government. He's in the Ministry of Defence.'

'Sounds good.'

'Yes.'

'I'll bet you get a fuller grant than Les.'

'Much.'

'I'll bet Father loves that,' said Charles Wilson, nodding at the political tee-shirt.

'It's my mother's.' He pulled a surprised face at her. 'When she was my age she smashed the bourgeoisie with the best of them.'

'If you can't smash 'em, join 'em.'

She turned away from him to look out of the window. There was still sunlight outside; the last shops were closing.

'I do philosophy,' he said.

She was quiet, as if ignoring him, then said, 'What for?'

'Forget it,' he said, held up his hand to stop further words or in mock surrender. But she went on.

'What I mean is, it's the sort of thing one would do anyway, the relevant bits at least. Why not do something useful: medicine, science, engineering?'

'They're useful, are they?'

'Absolutely.'

He stirred the soup. She had her back to him and he took his time looking at her. Her black hair was cut short so that he could see her ears. Even standing casually at the window, drinking, she looked solid and purposeful. He could not help but dislike her. She would get involved in projects and meetings, receive minutes and write reports, take time off to have children and then assert her rights and re-achieve and make a career and so on. 'Poor cow,' thought Charles.

He poured some of the soup into a mug. Mug in one hand,

slice of bread in the other he left her and went into the bathroom. Les Holland was reading. He looked up from the soapy water, threw the book on to the floor, reached for the mug and then the bread.

'Cheers.'

'Strange girl,' said Charles.

'She didn't half look after me last night. I woke up this morning in Barney's. Dead chuffed he was. Wouldn't give me any breakfast, not even a cup of tea. So I swiped some clothes while he was in the bathroom and legged it.' Les finished the bread and started sipping the soup. 'She's one of Barney's students. He was all ready to give her one, but I saved her and gave her one myself on his back lawn.'

'What, her, on the back lawn?'

'That's right. Bangs like a shit-house door.'

'You old softy.'

Les finished the soup. 'Good that,' he said and gave Wilson the mug.

'Give Barney a wide berth then,' said Charles.

'What for? I thought I might rub it in a bit. He was that bloody narky this morning.'

'No, it's not just that, Les. Remember, I robbed him as well.'

'Spot on. A lot? Give me that towel, will you?'

'I had his snuff boxes, well, three of them, and I found a hundred and fifty quid in an envelope in his desk drawer.'

Les stood up and rubbed his belly with the towel. 'Well, I feel better now. Where are the boxes?'

'I sold them this afternoon in Leeds. I got three hundred and twenty for them.'

'Dear oh dear.'

'Yes, I know but that's how it is. The money's in the building society. I've kept fifty quid each for spends.'

'He'll know it's us. Well, you; I was on the injured list. It's made me hungry, that soup.' Les stepped out of the bath and sat on the closed lid of the lavatory to dry his feet. 'Is she all right in there, what do they call her, Daphne?'

'Deborah,' Charles corrected him.

'That's right.'

'She's done an inventory of the flat, opened the wine, bollocked me for parasitism and lapsed into a self-contained silence.'

'You didn't see her on Barney's back lawn.' He stood up. 'Right, I'll get dressed. Then I've some money to pick up from the bookie's and we can go and have a pint and some dinner. Why not ring Celia up?' Les wrapped the towel round himself and walked out of the bathroom. He looked round the kitchen door. 'Just going to get dressed, love,' he said. Deborah turned from the window. 'We're going to the pub and we can have some dinner after. I can get to the betting shop as well if I hurry up.'

'No, I don't fancy the pub,' she said. 'What are you doing later?'

'Oh, come for a drink.'

'No,' she said, calmly, 'I'm going back to the university. Come up later, there's a disco.' She picked up her bag from the table. 'Bye,' she said and walked through the door and down the stairs. He watched her to the street and she was gone.

CHAPTER THREE

He could see the motes of dust in the pale light of the window. A smoke brown room. Charles Wilson drank his beer in the quietness, waiting for the door to open and let in the noise and clatter of the street.

'Hello mate, get you a drink?' Les Holland danced into the room. 'Fifty-eight pounds sixty.' He pulled out a handful of screwed-up notes and put them on the table. Charles laughed at him.

'Where did you get that?'

'On the dogs.'

'What do you know about dogs?'

'If you bet on their numbers when they're fives or multiples of five, see. It's Pythagorean.' Charles thought of Les, there, in the betting shop amongst the late-afternoon drinkers and men in shiny suits, the old lady drinking milky tea as she took their money from them.

'I'd keep dead quiet about this system, Les, especially in the bookie's.'

'It works, look.'

'Of course it does,' said Charles and drained his glass. 'Bitter please,' and he handed the glass to Les.

He heard Les ask for the beer and saw the fat landlady

begin to pull on the beer pumps; the white flesh hung down from the bone of her arm and quivered with the effort. Les went through a pantomime search of his pockets and turned, sharp with awkwardness at having forgotten the money on the table. He raised a finger. 'Sorry, just a minute,' and he stepped across to the table and smoothed out a note from the crumpled screw of money. 'Have one yourself, love?' he asked.

Then, at last, he was back with Charles.

'Put it away,' said Charles, glancing down at the money. 'Come on, before they come in and spend it for you.'

'Right,' said Les. He made a roll of the notes, leaned to one side on his chair and put them into his trouser pocket. He drank some beer, looked up at the room, moved his shoulders to some tune in his head. 'How's Celia?' he said abruptly. Charles cracked into a smile.

'She was all right this morning. Well, she was asleep when I left.' Then he said, 'Les?'

'What?'

'I think I've had enough of Celia.'

'Ah,' said Les, suddenly cheered. 'Mind if I have a bash at her?'

'You sympathetic little bastard.'

'What have I done?'

'I could be really hurt you know, having a really bad time.'

'Who? You? You've been running her around for months, poor cow.' Les was incredulous, then offended. 'Don't go criticising me.'

'All right,' said Charles, 'get along and do her a big favour. Show her a good time.'

'I shall.' Les got up and went to the fruit machine, started slotting in coins and punching at the yellow buttons. The machine thumped into a spasm of noise and coins clattered out, filling its trough and spilling on to the floor. There were ten pence and fifty pence coins; Les stacked them in one pound piles. 'It's another fifteen quid,' he said. 'Let's drink it here and then go up to the university.'

'I'd be sick.'

'Well, we could have gin or champagne.'

'Champagne,' said Charles disgustedly, 'they don't sell champagne in here.'

'Off licence then,' said Les, doggedly pursuing his idea. 'We could sit in the park with a couple of bottles.'

'Oh, shut up; go and get some more beer.'

'You're always doing that,' Les snarled at him from the bar. 'Two bitters, please.'

Charles turned. 'Oh, do be quiet, Les,' he said loudly.

Les flared, suddenly, into violence. 'Upper-class twat. Looking down your nose . . .'

'Hey, that's enough of that,' said the barmaid.

'And two large gins,' yelled Les at the top of his voice. She backed away. 'Come on then,' he said more quietly, but with anger still plain in his tone. She gave him the drinks and as he waited for his change he emptied the gins into the two pints of beer.

'It's nice with gin in it,' said Charles as they sat sipping their drinks. 'Have you tried it with lots of gin, half and half say?' Les took a big drink and reflected.

'No,' he said, 'too much that. Just put a bit of poke in it that's all.'

'A bit of sophistication,' said Charles Wilson.

CHAPTER FOUR

After the street and the sharp, clean sunlight, Celia stood thankfully behind the door in the cool secrecy of the old house. The walls were damp, the gloom cold and still. A brief, narrow hall led to a bare staircase. She turned to her left, kicked open the door; the sunlit kitchen was dirty and littered.

Below her the street was still and the parked cars on the opposite side gleamed. She sat in the open window. The old sash window was pushed right up and she could lean back against the frame and take the sunshine on her face. She closed her eyes and the light was red and heavy. Her breath grew lighter and she could feel against her breast the echo of her heartbeat.

There were no houses on the other side of the street; black cast iron railings, a steep cutting to two sets of railway lines.

She got down from the window and went into the front room of the flat. There were books and papers spread over the table by the bay window. It was a large room with a high, moulded ceiling. The floor was bare, polished wood. The only furniture was the small oak dining table and its four chairs. She loved the impression of space that she had whenever she entered the room, left deliberately empty

19

and magnified so that the space imposed itself upon anyone who entered. She sat. 'An hour,' she said aloud, 'and
then I'll eat something.' She looked at the words, tracked
back until she found her place and understood again what
she had done that afternoon.

It was still and silent. She sat, slightly bent, her hands
clasped under her breast.

Afterwards, her hour up, she stood watching her beef-
burger fry and thought about Charles, wanting him there
to argue away at her. She tried to turn her mind away from
him. She could not think that he had really gone and would
stay away. She wanted to talk to him about the work that
she had done that evening and it was so crass that he
should absent himself for some imagined hurt. She dipped
a bit of bread into the yolk of her egg and sat, thrilled, that
she had done the work; that great stack of words got
through, understood. 'I can do whatever I please to make
myself do,' she thought.

She put on a pullover on top of her dress and went out of
the flat, downstairs to the street. She was cold and walked
quickly to the main road where the bright lights drew her
into the bustle of traffic and people. She began to run as she
saw her bus coming in the line of vehicles, beat it to the stop
and sat down on the front seat upstairs.

Celia stood at the bar where the white light held steady
against the darkness and the sombre, startling flashes of the
light show in the disco. She drank the top inch of her cider
and backed out through the press of bodies into the twilit
noise. Her white dress picked up the light; she flickered and
vanished as she stood against the wall. An enormous boy
with a semi-shaven head was looking down at her, leaning

on the wall beside her, half turning so that he loomed over her. She turned, smiling, and touched him lightly. They stood trying to talk in the crashing noise.

'Charlie,' she shouted in the boy's ear and pointed into the lights. He twisted round to follow her gesture and there was Charles, turning round and round with Les clasped to him in a dramatic waltz, stately, in the reeling dancers around them. They changed to a sort of battleship tango and marched ruthlessly into the crowd at the bar.

Celia and the boy burst into laughter. She reached up and kissed him and then followed Charles to the bar.

He turned sharply and almost bumped into her. The excitement drained from his face and he closed his eyes as if in search of patience. His bland, cruel face enraged her suddenly, her pride rebelled at last. She saw faces turning to look as he said, 'Oh, piss off, Celia,' and she fell forward on to his chest and bit him in the soft flesh over his nipple, hard. He screamed and dropped his drink, she threw her cider at him glass and all and kicked him. The crowd at the bar were cheering and clapping.

Angry and satisfied she pushed through them, back to the boy with the crewcut; she hugged herself to his hard body, felt his great, meaty arms gently on her back.

'Pretty good, that,' said a girl's voice from behind her. She turned in the embrace and saw Deborah.

She was puzzled for a moment then said, 'You were with Les, last night at Barney's.' They stood looking at each other awkwardly.

Deborah put her hands in her trouser pockets and shrugged. 'It's not on with either of them, is it?' she said. She looked sad, near to tears.

'No, don't,' said the boy and reached out and took her by

the back of her neck and pulled her to him.

'James they call him,' said Celia.

'Stop it, Chas,' said Les Holland. He put his hand over the top of Charles's glass. 'No more drink, listen,' he said urgently. 'No, listen.' He gestured with his clenched fist and pulled Charles after him out of the lights and music, out into the cool, dark night.

'What's going on?' said Charles.

'No more drink. Are you pissed?'

'A bit.'

'Well, go and be sick. Go on and do it. Do it. I've found something for us. Next half hour.'

Charles went into the shrubbery and Les could hear him hawking and retching. He came back, sat on the ground and leaned against the concrete wall.

'That was dreadful,' he said.

'Listen, there are no alarms on the exhibition in Heslington Hall.'

'Oh dear,' said Charles, holding his head in his hands. 'I feel awful. What exhibition?'

'The Modernism exhibition.'

'Oh yes, load of crap I thought.'

Les spoke slowly, as if to an idiot. 'They have not alarmed it.'

Charles sat quietly with his head on his knees. His voice came up muffled. 'It's a rush. What about a car? We'd need a van,' he said stupidly.

'No, you dick, we can't take all of it,' shouted Les. Then he knelt beside Charles and whispered, 'There's one thing, a painting. It must be twenty thousand plus.'

'How do you know it doesn't have an alarm?'

'I've been in the bar over there . . .'

'What for?'

'For a walk; but listen, the porters were going on about it. How daft it was.'

'How can we get in?'

'The Hall's open till ten, it's twenty to ten now. If they catch us we can say it's just a jolly student jape. The prats would believe us.'

'We'll need a car.'

'No time, come on.'

They walked up the flight of stone steps at the front of the Hall and in through the front door. It was brightly lit and eerily empty. They walked up the main staircase and into the large, still room. Across its centre there were portable screens which held pictures. They peeped round them; there was no one. Les walked to the end of the room where a portrait of an angular, long-faced woman hung.

'Do you think there is an alarm?' said Les.

'Les, please.'

Les picked the painting off the wall. It was just small enough to go under his arm, but still cumbersome. They could not stop themselves running as they went down the steps and into the gloom of the shrubbery.

'What should we do now?' Les whispered.

'Get the frame off it anyway.'

'We can ring for a taxi then.'

'No, no,' said Charles. 'We'll hide it. Then we'll watch them lock the Hall up and see if it's missed. Then we'll stay late at the disco and then we'll ring for a taxi.'

CHAPTER FIVE

'Hundred and fifty quid,' said Bernard Guy and slapped his hand on the worktop. A dead potted plant his wife had left jumped and rattled. He went through the jars marked 'Flour', 'Sugar', 'Salt' until he found his cash card. 'Little sods.'

He went into the living room and switched on the television, sat drinking cans of lager and watched the tail end of a cricket match. Barney was almost fifty years old and beginning to puff up into the fat in which old athletes lose themselves.

'House's filthy,' he thought, 'should get a cleaning lady.' The thought of his wife came to him. His third had left him the previous Christmas. All three had left him and left him finally flat-footed and lethargic, crumbling under his inability to persuade anyone else into his bed. He reached over for the tobacco jar on the coffee table and rolled himself a joint. He sat smoking and drinking and watched the cricket.

When he awoke it was almost dark and at first he thought that he was in bed but then he heard the television. He felt grimy and cold. In the kitchen he threw some cold water on his face, wiped himself on a tea towel; noticing that it smelled he dropped it on the floor in front of the washing machine.

Alan Smith

It was after nine o'clock and Barney walked through the warm twilight, past the Minster, under the old stone gateway and into the town.

'Couple of pints and some dinner,' he thought.

The casino was a gleaming, plush red. There was smoke and a taut hum of voices. It was turned three and Barney was dizzy with drink and tiredness. He perched on a stool and a dark, tubercular girl flipped cards across to him, intent and defensive and took his money. Barney watched the girl, shiny black hair over a white stretched face. She flipped a card to the man on his right; another card and then she looked at him. A card landed in front of him, two of clubs. He tapped the table; another card, a picture. He pushed the cards away with the back of his hand and stood as the girl picked up cards and chips with the polished spatula.

He walked away from the table a couple of paces and stood vacantly, there being no reason to move in one direction rather than another. The cigarette packet in his jacket was empty so he went to the buffet table where there were cigarettes stuffed in wine glasses for the gamblers. As he was there he ate a couple of sandwiches and asked the barman for a whisky. A couple of yards in front of him were the backs of the people around the roulette table; the middle-aged ones sober, the young ones drunk. Now that he had no money left at all he felt quite detached. He noticed how heavily serious the sober ones were and how less foolish it was, in this setting at least, to be a drunk. He felt himself tottering a bit as he turned back to the buffet.

'A whisky, please,' he said, with a drunk's massive politeness and the young man handed him a new glass and took the empty one from him. Barney saw the sleek face go in and

26

out of focus a couple of times. 'Ho, ho,' he thought.

'Pardon,' said the young man. Barney looked at him, but it took an increasing effort to stop him slipping away.

'Ho, ho,' said Barney. He wagged his finger over the buffet, drained his glass and turned for the door. The turn was too sudden; he tottered a few paces until the wall stopped him. Then the door was open and he could feel someone's grip on his upper arm.

'Out you go, sunshine,' said a voice and he was pushed forward. He took a couple of steps and managed not to fall on to the pavement. Then there were no more voices; the air was cool and smokeless. The door shut behind him.

'Buggery,' said Barney.

He looked up and down the street. Some of the shop windows were lit and the street lighting gleamed, sodium white, on the smooth paving slabs. Barney walked slowly up the gentle slope of the street until it led him to the square where the Minster loomed sepulchrally ahead. When he reached the steps leading to its main doors he sat and fished around in his pockets for one of the loose cigarettes from the casino. He lay back, leaning on his elbows, smoking.

Out there in the blackness someone was pulling at his foot. Barney kicked out and tried to turn over to a more comfortable position, but he bumped down, jarringly, on to something hard. Then he was in the street again with the lamps and the Minster. An old man was pulling at his left shoe and growling. He saw the matted hair and filthy half beard, the greasy raincoat and he kicked out in panic. The old man stepped back and growled at him, scrabbled once more at his feet as Barney kicked again and, lying on his back, tried to retreat up the Minster steps.

'Get off,' he shouted, shivering with revulsion, shaking as

he felt the hands on his leg. There was another shout and running and the scrabbling hands were gone.

'Right, get up, you,' said the policeman. Barney sat up and hunched, shivering, on the cold stone. 'Come on,' said the policeman and rapped Barney's head a couple of times with the back of his hand.

'Hang on, hang on,' said Barney, 'I feel terrible.' He began to slip back into sleep, started to topple over, lurched back into wakefulness with the thin taste of sick in his mouth. 'Sick,' he said. The policeman pulled him to his feet and ran him down the steps to the edge of the pavement. Barney knelt by the gutter and vomited.

'Can't have you spewing on the Minster, pal. Come on, I'll get you tucked up for the night.'

'No, no,' said Barney, shivering. 'Get home okay; ten minutes.' The policeman pulled him to his feet once more, took a big handful of his jacket and held him against a street lamp. Barney felt the world slip away, blank and indifferent.

Then he was sitting in a smell of polish and cigarettes and someone was lifting his legs.

'Get bloody in, Barney,' said someone. He floundered around, felt his hand on a face. 'Get off,' said the same voice.

Barney sat still and thought, 'Who's that? I know that voice.'

'Hurry up,' said the policeman. The doors banged.

They were searching him.

'Nothing, not a cent.'

'Get his keys then.'

The sun shone brightly through the open curtains. Bernard Guy grimaced against the glare and the wretchedness he felt. He looked around his bedroom, fearing the worst.

Alarm clock, was it? He shut his eyes and the waves of dizziness made him tense and sickly. A great gush of sorrowfulness hit him. Then the ringing again.

It was the doorbell; it rang again and again, a long piercing shrill from the foot of the stairs. Barney sat up; he was dressed. His limbs itched and ached in the sweaty cloth. The sound of the doorbell came at him again. He got out of bed and stood up. It caught him beautifully, just as he reached the door it screamed out next to his ear. At the door stood Les Holland and Charles Wilson.

'Get out of it,' said Barney. 'Where's my money?'

'At least be pleasant, Barney, let us in,' said Les. 'I've got some of your clothes here.' He held up a carrier bag. Barney took the bag and made to close the door.

'Get home all right?' asked Charles. Barney paused.

'Here I am,' he said.

'Only just,' said Charles, rising angrily.

'Knock it off, Chas,' said Les. Then he drawled, 'We found you, didn't we? You were being arrested and we rescued you. To tell the truth, old Clive was glad to see the back of you.'

'Who's Clive?'

'The chap who was arresting you,' said Charles. 'He goes in the Falcon.'

'Lucky me,' said Barney nastily and walked back into the kitchen, leaving the door open. Les and Charles followed him into the kitchen. 'We were going home and saw you lolling around by the Minster and as Clive hadn't quite got around to his arrest he let us put you in our cab.' Charles was full of patience and charm as he explained.

'What about my hundred and fifty pounds?' said Barney.

'Thanks, lads, I'm really grateful,' said Les. 'That's all right, Barney, any time.'

'Look, I need the money. Go and steal from somebody rich.'

'You're rich,' explained Les.

'It was you, you admit it.'

'No, we don't,' said Les. He looked round at the machines, the fitted kitchen. 'You're rich, look at it all. Rooms full of rich in your house, Barney.'

'What are you doing?' said Barney to Charles.

'He's making coffee,' said Les.

'Well, make tea.' Barney sat down and leaned forward over the kitchen table. They stood and looked at him while they waited for the kettle to boil. 'What do you want?' he asked.

'Why do you think you're not rich?' Charles asked him quietly.

'Three wives and four children.'

'How not rich are you?'

'Come on, Chas,' said Les. 'He's got a bloody great salary, writes books, and look at this place.'

'Listen, you,' said Barney, flaring at him, 'divide by two three times and pay out for four kids.' He drank his tea and shivered. There was silence.

'Well, as long as you're all right,' said Charles, 'we'll be off.' Les raised his hand in farewell. Barney stood up, sheepish.

'Yes, okay. Thanks for asking, boys, and for last night.' He stood up. 'Look,' he said more firmly, 'the hundred and fifty . . .'

'Not us, man,' said Les.

Barney punched down on to the table. 'I need it.' His voice was quiet.

Les and Charles walked out of the kitchen and closed the door. Barney sat again at the table. The front door didn't slam; he waited, then got up.

They came back into the room. 'You really are in the shit?' asked Les.

'They'll believe him, I tell you,' said Charles. 'Now, with us they'll neither believe nor disbelieve, just turn us inside out as a matter of course. They'll come into our flat any time, but Barney is a professor, well nearly, and they don't know the difference. He's got a big house and so on. They'll listen to him, worry about the consequences, but, above all, for my money, they'll not believe that he'd do it.'

'That's because you're a posh kid, Chas. Even now you're surprised when one of them isn't polite to you. You'll see when they arrive at the flat and get stuck in. They believe nobody.'

They were through the town centre and away from the big shops and department stores. They walked up Micklegate past the terraces of smaller, older shops towards their flat. The street was confined suddenly by the malicious old stone of Micklegate Bar.

'Look, all that crap about class . . .'

'Ask my dad,' said Les, ignoring him.

'I'd ask him nothing,' said Charles derisively. 'They keep on catching him.' Les stopped and caught hold of Charles's arm, hard, so that he pulled up sharply.

'That's it. All right?' He stabbed his forefinger at Charles. Charles shook his arm free. They looked at each other for a second and walked on in silence.

They got to the door and Charles had the key in the lock when the two men stood up close behind them.

'Good morning,' said the small thin one. 'Mr Wilson, Mr Holland?'

'That's right,' said Charles. He saw the warrant card. 'Oh,

31

officer; how might we help you?' A suburban public school boy.

'Shut it,' said the big, blank man. Without looking round he waved his hand in the air. They heard four car doors slam and they were pushed into the gloomy hallway.

Les sat in the kitchen doing his best to look surprised. He let Charles bluster. The two detectives who had met them at the door stayed with them in the kitchen while the other four men went through the rooms of the flat.

'This is absolutely shocking,' said Charles, wonderfully bewildered. Then, as if struck suddenly by a saving line, 'Your warrant. Show me your search warrant or you must leave now.'

'Shut it,' said the big blank man. He dropped a heavy white hand on to Charles's shoulder and he sank beneath its weight on to a kitchen chair. Charles started to look afraid and cast his eyes around in panic as if searching for help.

'Give over,' sneered the small thin man. 'We know.'

'What?' said Charles and Les together. The big man gripped a handful of Charles's hair and Charles saw his other fist bulging. The panic was real and then his hair was released. He looked at the thin man who smiled at the fear plain in his face.

The thin man placed his finger on Charles's lips and said, 'Shh.'

The other four came crowding into the kitchen. As they were leaving the thin man said, 'We know. We do.' And they were gone.

There was a silence and then Les said, 'Well, you were surprised, weren't you?'

'No,' said Charles.

'Bollocks.'

They looked around the flat. It looked as though they had moved in that day and the removals men had just left. Everything was out of place but neatly so, in piles, moved to one side or not hanging on the wall.

'See,' explained Les, 'they don't know at all.'

'Neat, aren't they?' said Charles. 'Why don't they?'

'Well, it's very respectful isn't it? No breakages. What could we complain of? You are going to complain, Chas, aren't you?'

'Should we?'

'You should. They'll expect that; me, well, they'll think I'm used to it. They'll know about my lot.' He sat on Charles's bed and picked up the bottle of rum from the floor. He took a drink and passed the bottle to Charles. 'Get in touch with your tutor.'

'That prick.'

'No, that's what you'd do if you were really you; public school, army family, all terribly terribly.' He saw Wilson's glare. 'But, as you're not at all like that,' he went on, teasing, 'you ought to work all the harder at being exactly like that.'

'You can forget it. It doesn't matter. I'm not going to do any of that; tutors, solicitors, complaints. Sod it; what's the point of being a criminal if you still go through all that shit?'

'Suit yourself.'

'That's the point isn't it?'

Bernard Guy put the picture back on the wall. He liked that one. It was a poster, Andrew Wyeth's Old Boot. He straightened the frame and stood back. He could feel the excitement mounting, fluttering in his stomach, wanting to tell, gossip, impress.

'None of that,' he thought. 'A thousand quid, a thousand quid. Very useful that would be.'

CHAPTER SIX

Celia woke up. The first thing she thought was, 'Charlie,' and then she felt the unusual, starched sheet and the body cramped against her back. 'Deborah,' she said, remembering. She felt Deborah's hand on her breast, tracing lightly across her stomach. She sat up and looked around the room. The hand touching her thigh. The sun was shining through blue woollen curtains on to the books, showing up the dust on the dead television screen. 'It's hot in here,' she said.

'There's tea on the desk. I think that the kettle's full,' said Deborah. She lay looking at Celia's back, rolled over in the bed and kissed her spine.

Celia twisted to look over her shoulder. 'Oh no,' she said lightly and stood up. 'Where's the nearest shower?'

'Almost opposite, a bit to the right. You should get a room in college.'

'Oh, all these students.'

'That's what we are, isn't it?'

Celia wrapped Deborah's blanket around herself and picked up a towel from the back of the desk chair. 'No,' she said and closed the door behind her.

The coffee bar was open and they sat eating toast and

yoghurt in the low, open sprawl of the common room. The walls were off-white, posters and paintings, worn airport armchairs, scratched tables. There was a jaded silence, a hint of stale beer and tobacco in the air. They both looked up at the clatter of feet and strident voices.

A group of seven or eight men, two of them in police uniforms, peaked hats covered in silver, walked past them and banged through the outer doors towards Heslington Hall.

'Vice Chancellor,' said Deborah. She got up and went to the door through which they had gone. She stood, staring through the glass for some moments, then shouted, childishly excited, 'Vans and cars, blue lights,' and beckoned urgently. Celia skipped over to her and stood, still eating her toast, looking at the busy lights and bad-tempered men.

'Come on,' said Deborah. They pushed through the doors and walked along the paved way, past the vans and across the wide meadow of lawn towards the bustle.

There were a few students standing on the lawn, watching. 'What's up?' said Deborah to a tall, young man in a yellow track suit.

'Burglars, I think,' he said. They both looked at him in disgust.

'Don't be pathetic,' said Deborah. 'What burglars? What's been pinched?'

Celia had walked off, was making for the front door of the Hall. Unlike the rest of the university it was old; an old country house with wide, stone steps leading to an arched entry. She was almost in the shadow of the porch when the constable stopped her.

'Sorry, miss,' he said. He was her own age, pink and soft under the sudden, abrasive blue of his uniform. She ignored him and had almost brushed past when he caught hold of her arm. Oddly he took her by the wrist, almost as if he were trying to hold her hand. She half turned and looked at him. He stood awkwardly. 'Can't go in there this morning,' he said, briskly. Celia stood, smiling, enjoying his uncertainty.

'Show us your policeman's helmet,' said Deborah slyly, sidling up to him.

'Bugger off,' he said, grinning at them. He dropped Celia's arm and waved them away. 'Unless you want a taste of my truncheon.'

'You rude thing,' said Celia. 'What's been stolen?'

'A painting,' he said. 'Now go on, push off.' They ran down the steps, turning to blow kisses at him.

When they got back to the common room their coffee cups had gone, the table was wiped. They bought two more coffees and sat in the scarred armchairs.

'He was nice,' said Deborah.

'The policeman?'

'No, last night.' Deborah smiled, salaciously. 'James.'

'Oh yes,' said Celia, as if she had half forgotten.

'Do you have him as well as Charles?'

'Sort of,' said Celia. 'Hard to explain, really. I suppose that he's my big, fleshy fantasy.'

'May I have him too?' asked Deborah.

'You did, I was there, remember?'

CHAPTER SEVEN

Mary Wilton hated pushing the trolley into Wayne Barker's suite. The last time he had put his hand up her skirt and squeezed the back of her thigh. The time before that he had stroked her arm. 'Little twat,' she thought. Mary Wilton was twenty-one; she had two children and lived with her mother. She went through the door and said to Wayne Barker, 'Supper, Mr Barker.'

Wayne Barker was forty-two, muscular, fat and squat. He had a small nose, meaty cheeks bruised with blood pressure and a dark shadow of beard.

'Right,' he said, 'go on then.'

Mary Wilton went; next time she'd spit in the soup. Barker looked at his supper, poked at the fish, picked up a piece of tomato from the salad and ate it. He pulled the trolley over to the television and stood eating, watching the evening news. They mentioned his painting, briefly, towards the end. There was no mention of his name; the man talked about 'a valuable painting'. There was a brief picture of some of the university buildings, a bit of lake and some talk about the police.

He picked up the phone and said the number he wanted.

'Graham,' he said, 'yes, it's me. Now then, who do we

know up here?' He listened and then, his voice raised, 'Never mind bloody journalists, what about a policeman, are there any of them that we know? Well, send Ellis up here. Have him here first thing tomorrow. Oh yes, find out what it's worth, this painting.'

He lay back on the bed and flicked through the television channels. He was reading the brochure advertising dirty videos when Mary Wilton knocked on the door and came into the room.

'Have you finished?' she asked.

'Take it.' He watched her cross the room. As she was backing towards the door with the trolley he said, 'Do you want to earn twenty pounds?'

She stood up straight, her hands on her hips and said, hostile, 'Fifty.'

Eric Ellis turned sideways on the bench, away from the river. He turned his face up to the sun and then, as if its warmth had softened him, he said, 'Listen here, Sergeant Devonshire, I was a copper for years and years and I know.' Devonshire looked woodenly back at him. 'There's no question of wrong-doing, just a few extras.'

'Like what?'

'Like telling me what's going on. Telling me who's the favourite or if there are any deals in the offing with the insurance and so on.'

'What for?'

'What for, you pillock. Do you know what this silly bloody picture turns out to be worth? Course you don't. Nearly a hundred thousand. Now, my boss, he doesn't want deals, he doesn't want higher premiums, he doesn't want to look a soft touch.'

'What does he want?'

'He wants his picture. To be frank, though, I'd say he wants a spot of revenge as well. Nothing wild, you know, a few teeth, a few ribs.'

'I'm not getting into all that,' said Robert Devonshire. 'The odd phone call I don't mind.'

'You'll not lose by it. I'm going to be around for a few days. Let you know what I find out, shall I, Sergeant?'

Eric Ellis was a short, wiry man. He was neat in dark suits and starched collars; dark hair oiled back from his small face.

He tapped with his knuckles on the counter at the porters' lodge. 'Shop,' he shouted and brought out the fat, red-faced porter.

'Hello then,' said the porter putting his mug of milky tea between them. Ellis nodded at the empty room behind the fat man.

'I wonder if we could have a more private word?'

'Is it this painting?' said the porter in annoyance. 'I've had the police round, you know. Did I see this, did I see that. Where was I, what time, was it light enough to see?'

'I'll bet,' said Ellis, smiling sympathetically. 'They take up your time without a thank you. I wouldn't like you to imagine that's my way. I'd like to conduct a proper, private interview in a reasonable and professional manner with a proper financial acknowledgement of your cooperation.'

When they were sitting in the fat porter's office with the door shut he said to Ellis, 'I'd put money on two of them little bastards. Saw 'em rolling around the bushes; being sick, one was.'

'It doesn't sound too promising.'

'Coppers thought that as well, then they went off and

found out a bit about them and they soon came back. Pair of clever little bastards. That Charlie Wilson especially, bloody trouble maker.'

'Who do you think that the police spoke to to give them such an interest?'

'Oh, Frank Vernon.'

'Who's he?'

'Wilson's supervisor. Right miserable bastard he is.'

'This Vernon, what's he supposed to do when he supervises?'

The fat porter leaned across to Ellis and tapped his arm. 'One thing about that Charlie Wilson, at least he's not a poofter, anything but. I reckon that's why Vernon has it in for him. Bloody pervert. Drop Charlie in it he would, take pleasure in it,' said the fat porter putting the twenty pound note into his top pocket.

'It's the second door on the right,' said the typist and smiled at him. Ellis went down the narrow corridor, tapped once on the door and opened it. The large, bare face looked up, grimacing in annoyance.

'Yes, what?' said Frank Vernon. Ellis looked for a few seconds at the bony head, scraped white nose, hanging over the desk. Ellis took out his wallet and from it gave Vernon a business card.

'I'm no wiser,' said Vernon, cattily, and pushed the card back across the desk.

Eric Ellis imagined taking Vernon by his pale, ginger hair and ramming his nose into the desk. He put his hands in his pockets and leaned back on the door so that it shut behind him.

'Barker's Media Systems,' he explained. 'And, as far as this place is concerned, Barker's Exhibition Centre.' He sat down across the desk from Vernon.

'Well,' said Vernon. 'What about it?'

'Mr Vernon,' said Eric Ellis, ironically patient, 'if you don't help me, if you don't stop bullshitting, if you don't stop pretending that you don't know what's going on, then I shall become quite cross with you. I shall go to the Vice Chancellor and tell him what a big shit bag you are and that my employer could not possibly build his big posh building here because there are lecturers here who turdburgle the students and that these lecturers are called Frank Vernon.'

It was one o'clock when Ellis left Frank Vernon's office. He walked through Derwent College, past the fat porter at the door and into the car park.

Robert Devonshire's wife woke him up. 'It's for you,' she said and pointed towards the living room door.

'What?' he said, bewildered.

'Telephone.' She switched off the television. 'Go on.'

Devonshire rubbed his face, looked at his watch. 'Who is it?' he asked. She shrugged.

'Sergeant Devonshire? Eric Ellis here. I've had a look round at the university and I've a name for you. There's a student called Charles Wilson.'

Devonshire made him wait while he wrote down the name. Then, coming to his senses, he said, 'You've been talking to that porter. We've been round to Wilson's place, it's in Micklegate, there's nothing there.'

'Course there's not. Now look, you just keep at Wilson, keep on popping up, you know what to do. I reckon that he might get fed up and give us back that picture.'

43

Devonshire hesitated, then said, 'Ellis, there's his mate as well, a kid called Holland.'

'I know. Thanks for telling me anyway. Chase them round a bit, Robert; they're only students.'

CHAPTER EIGHT

Even in his light summer suit Roy Holland was too hot. He bent and pulled at the stick, but the dog clamped his teeth hard and shook his head. He threw the stick, whirling across the park and the labrador pounded after it.

'Bloody Les and his bloody mates,' he said out loud. It was early and Abington Park was empty; he headed towards the lake, worrying away at what to do about his son. He sat on a bench and watched the ducks. The dog lay at his feet, looking up at him.

'I thought he'd be bloody set up,' he told the dog. 'University, bloody A levels. Bloody English, you might know. He could have been a bloody accountant, a solicitor.' He picked up the dog's stick and hurled it into the lake. The dog crashed in after it. 'You've more bloody sense.'

Roy Holland got up from the bench and walked up the grassy slope to Wellingborough Road, the dog trailed after him stopping twice to shake the water from itself before it caught up.

'He wants me to sell a bloody painting for him, Mick. I don't know about paintings.' He put the lead on the dog and they crossed the road.

'You've had him in that lake,' said his wife Susan when she

saw the dog. Mick woofed at her, once. 'Take him outside, go on you,' she said to her husband.

'Come on then, you poor old bugger,' said Roy. He opened the kitchen door and pushed the dog out into the back garden. He sat down at the table and his wife put a cup of tea in front of him. 'She's beautiful,' he thought. He turned to look at her, her red hair and pale skin that was freckled now with the sun. 'You look sixteen,' he said softly. She tutted.

'Drink your tea,' she said. 'What time is that shop going to open this morning?'

'I'll open at nine, as usual. What about Les? Is he up?'

'Leave him, love,' said Susan. 'I'll send him on later; they were in late last night, him and Charlie.'

'Pissed,' said Roy Holland.

'How much bacon do you want?'

'A lot and two eggs. How about some fried bread?' He put his hand on her hip as she brushed past him to get to the cooker.

'You'll get no fried bread from me, it's bad for you.' She knocked his hand away, but then stroked his head, flattening his hair forward. 'You're going bald, you old sod,' she said and kissed him. 'If I'm cooking for you, you'd better go and get those two up, I suppose. Tell them they can have eggs and bacon now or what they get themselves later on.'

In Les Holland's bedroom the sunlight had already woken Les and Charles; they listened to Roy coming up the stairs. They had split the bed and Charles was lying on the floor on the mattress.

'Morning,' said Roy as he came into the room. 'Your mum's doing a fry up but you've got to come now.'

'Good morning, Roy,' said Charles Wilson.

'I feel terrible, Dad,' said Les. Roy sat down on the bed and kissed his son on the forehead.

'You bloody stink an' all. Go on, get washed and don't let your mother see that you're bad.'

'Where're my trousers?' said Les.

'Your mother's binned them,' said Roy, 'and your jacket. Have a good story for her when you get down, she found nearly eighty quid in the pockets.'

'It was a good suit, that.' He kicked Charles who was still lying on the floor. 'What's funny, then?' Charles and Roy grinned at each other.

Roy said, 'There's all clean in the wardrobe for you. Come on, it'll be getting cold.'

The three of them ate Susan's big breakfast and Roy left to open his shop. They heard his car door slam. Susan turned on Les.

'Where did you get seventy-eight pound?' Her face was pinched with anxiety and anger.

'Not in front of a guest, Mam.'

'Guest, my arse, Leslie.'

'All right, I cleared my account in York. I thought it could go into a building society.'

'You, a building society?'

'It's good interest,' he said to her, weathering her disbelief. She turned to the pots in the sink. Les grinned at Charles behind her back.

'And you can stop pulling faces, Leslie Holland,' she snapped.

At half past nine on a Saturday morning Roy Holland's small jewellery shop was empty.

'Another half hour and they'll be fighting to get in,' he told Charles. 'Silly buggers can't spend it quick enough.' They were sitting around his small workbench in the cramped back room.

'Roy,' said Charles, 'this painting of ours, how can we sell it?'

'I don't really know, Charlie, son. The only people I ever knew who did things for collectors took orders in advance. Unless you take a big beating on the price you're going to be stuck with it.'

'Well, it was a windfall anyway, Dad,' said Les.

'That's no attitude to take,' said Roy sharply. 'It's not a bleedin' game this, you know. Look, lads,' he said, 'I don't know why you're in this. You can get nice degrees and nice jobs and generally make a fortune. If you take one fall at this, the economics come apart. You're better off carrying bricks about and digging holes and all that.'

'It's not what you think it is, Dad,' said Les.

'It's not what you've ever dreamt of, son,' said Roy quietly, shaking his head. 'Nearly a year for me last time. If they pulled you in York you'd probably start with a few months in Armley, up in Leeds. Get on a train and go up there one afternoon and look at it. Just from the outside. Misery.'

'Roy.' Charles Wilson leaned forward between Les and his father. 'Like this we can decide what we do. We don't have to ask anybody for permission. We decide what to do and do it; we're in nobody's hands.'

'You're in everybody's hands: mine, the cops', anybody's. This is the most exposed way . . .' He stopped, seeing that he had lost them. 'Go on then, Les, you tell me.'

Les cast around for a moment. 'It's being on the outside, feeling separate, knowing that you've taken a real step, a real alternative . . .'

'You mean it's exciting, don't you?' interrupted his father, flatly.

'That's right. But it's what it's not, Dad, that's the important thing.' He pointed at his father. 'Look at you, you're full of bounce and cheek, aren't you? How many round here are like that? Round here in these offices and shops. You're nearly fifty, aren't you, and you're still Jack the lad and you're wanting me to line up for boredom and arsehole creeping in some manky office.' His voice rose, almost in anger, as he finished.

'Well, do something else then, son,' said Roy quietly, anxiety painful in his voice. 'But look, you and Charlie, you've got to stop this. This painting might give you a bit of capital.'

'Some people, though, Roy,' said Charles Wilson, 'the temptation to shit on them . . .'

'Do it safely, then. There's not a thing wrong with safety. When you're safe you can laugh. Try laughin' when you're banged up with two other fellers and one pot to piss in.' Then, awkwardly, confidentially, 'Look, this painting, have you thought about selling it back? You can do that you know. Insurance companies do it to cut their losses.' He paused and then plunged. 'I know a guy, well, I used to know him, who was a kind of a go-between . . .'

Charles and Les burst out laughing.

'From years ago,' protested Roy, hastily. 'Well, I still know him, but I don't use him. I don't, you little buggers.'

They spent the morning in the Central Library.

'Bloody clever this, you know,' said Les and he ran the mouse around, found Twentieth Century and clicked it.

'Modernism,' said Charles disgustedly.

'Right then,' said Les and clicked away a couple of times.

'This is more like it, Les.' On the screen were eight tiny representations of portraits and Dutch houses. Les started clicking through them.

'Journeyman stuff, that's all this is,' he said.

'If we'd managed to steal one of these, instead of that spiteful bastard, what's his name?' said Charles, belligerently, feigning forgetfulness.

'Wyndham Lewis.'

'Wyndham Lewis. Well then, there'd be no question of selling. I mean, you can't put the Vorticists or Francis bloody Bacon on the wall, can you? Who needs a wall full of ideas, particularly nasty ideas, when you're eating your dinner or watching the television? It would be like having someone read "The Proceedings of the Aristotelian Society" in the background all the time.'

'They're not that kind of painting,' said Les quietly, refusing to rise for once. 'Art's not that simple.'

'Not for looking at, isn't it?'

'Silly boy.'

'No,' said Charles sententiously. 'Art needs at least a foothold in nature.'

'Who says,' said Les, provoked at last by Charles's tone.

'Well, actually,' said Charles, with a small, mocking grin, 'it was Wyndham Lewis.'

'Sharpshit.'

'No, I'm telling you: literature, your racket, is for stories, art is for nature and philosophy is for ideas. If you mix them up then it's a mediocre mess. That's what Celia says and for once the silly cow's right.' He got up and walked away from Les in an attempt to end the conversation, but Les continued, raising his voice to bridge the distance between them and send the words echoing across the quiet, hunched desks.

'She's all right, your Celia. You want to get back in there while you can.'

'I'll always be able to,' Charles shouted back. Then, louder, 'She's a spaniel.'

The high room echoed with the noise and brought the librarian, an old man in a blue suit, red sunburned forehead, grey, thinning hair.

'Not falling out, are we, chaps?' he asked.

'Beg your pardon,' said Les. 'Bit of a row about your computer.' Charles walked back to the desk and smiled at him.

'Oh, those bloody things,' he said and left them to it.

Les clicked his way back to the Modernists. 'What do you reckon it's worth?'

'Our Wyndham Lewis? It's got to be quite a lot; more than twenty thousand, say.'

'We might get five then,' said Les, glumly. 'Promised Barney a grand. A bit crummy really.'

'Have they any on this?'

'They've got everything on here, pal.' They found a painting by Wyndham Lewis, another portrait, and sat looking at it.

'He was a funny sod,' said a voice from behind them. They turned to see the sunburned librarian. 'Argued with every bugger, put his kids in a workhouse, thought he was a genius, he did. Big-headed bastard.' ·

'Know about him do you?' asked Les.

'Oh yes.'

'How come?'

'I can read, you know.'

'Well, anyway,' said Charles, quickly butting in, 'he's fashionable now? Collectable?'

51

'Oh yes, rather, worth a bomb,' said the old man.

'What, that?' said Les, feigning disbelief.

'That,' said the man. 'I reckon they'd get seventy or eighty thousand quid for that. Fucking stupid,' he finished, scathingly.

'Oh, I think it's quite nice,' said Charles Wilson.

CHAPTER NINE

Les Holland's mother drank Carling Specials. She was standing at the bar with Charles Wilson pouring her third one.

'What about Celia, then, Charlie?'

'Well, Susan, no more Celia, I'm afraid.' Charles covered his face in his pint glass. They were pushed up close in the Saturday night press.

'Shame that,' said Susan, ignoring his reluctance to talk about Celia. 'Dead posh, Celia,' she said reflectively.

'Like me, you mean?'

'Oh no,' said Susan, 'not like you a bit. I know you talk funny like her, but you're common, you are.' She saw his face drop in surprise. 'I didn't mean it nasty,' she said, putting her hand on his shoulder. She searched for a way to comfort him, laughing in his face as she did so. 'Ah, come on, love, it's true isn't it? You fit in here all right, don't you, with this lot? And some right buggers get in here, you know.'

'They're all right.'

'There you are, you see. You and my Les, my Roy as well come to that, you get on well, don't you? Now, what I liked about Celia was that she stuck out like a sore thumb. Everybody was a bit more polite. She made this rabble feel a bit edgy like. She made me feel like getting my fish knives out.

She didn't mean to, if she had, it wouldn't have worked.'

'She's a pest. She clings. She's for ever . . .'

'Love, isn't it?'

'Oh, come on Susan.'

'Bloody right one, you are. Some poor buggers have feelings you know. We're not all like you, curling your sodding lip . . .'

'I've never curled it at you.'

'I'd split it for you if you did.'

'Exactly, and that's why Celia pisses me off.'

'Come on, clever, pick that tray of drinks up and let's get back to Roy and Les. My husband will think you're after me.'

'I am.'

'And me a grandma.' He stood, looking at her in disbelief. 'It's right,' she said and picked up the tray herself. 'Eighteen when I married Roy. Just done my A levels and he' – she nodded over at Roy – 'drops me in it. And now I'm a granny.' She saw the question coming and said, 'Forty.'

Early Sunday evening, Les and Charles sat in the train going back to York.

'We could be business men,' said Les.

'Or a nightclub,' said Charles. 'Something really sordid.'

'No, no,' said Les, oddly serious. 'Dad's right, we've got to stop wanting just to spit in people's eyes; we've got to concentrate on making money.' He turned to look at his friend. 'Now listen . . .'

'Yes,' said Charles and leaned forward, attentive, mocking.

'Stop being a kid, Chas. You can't just decide to be free or independent or whatever, you've got to finance it as well.'

'Well?'

'Well, there's got to be a bit more discipline . . .'

'You, discipline, you?' Charles's astonishment stung.

'I'm disciplined.' Les was self-righteous, indignant to the point of anger.

'You're a wreck. Disciplined?' Charles laughed. 'You're forever pissed, you gamble, you're into other people's women, without realising what you're doing . . .'

'Well, you're bloody wrong there pal. I might do all that, but I do it because I decide to do it. That's being disciplined, isn't it, deciding to do and then doing?'

'Not deciding to get pissed, you fool. That's not a decision.'

'It is.'

'Of course it isn't.'

'It is.'

'It isn't.'

Back in York they sat in the Falcon facing each other across a polished table, Charles with his back to the busy room. Roy Holland had finally worried them. He had nagged at them remorselessly through the weekend until Charles Wilson began to listen to the anguished love Roy felt for his son.

'Your father's perfectly right, of course,' he said to Les.

'Well, he worries about us.'

'He worries about you.'

'No, no, he likes you and my mother does.' Charles did not reply. 'That's shut you up, hasn't it?' said Les. 'Can't cope, can you? Bit of bloody affection and you shit yourself. Like poor old Celia. And your mum and dad,' he went on recklessly, 'what about them?'

'My mum and dad?' said Charles, and he turned to face Les. 'Before I was seven I was in boarding school and lucky to see them in the holidays. Pair of bastards.'

'Seven?' said Les, but Charles kept silent and Les let the minutes pass. He could think of nothing to say, such an abandonment out of his understanding. Finally, he pushed himself into saying, 'Well then, we'd better go and see Barney; tell him he'll have to wait a bit.'

'Offer him a bonus though, Les,' Charles began, stopping as he saw Les's eyes looking beyond him into the room.

'Shut it,' Les said softly, not moving his lips. Charles felt the weight of a hand on his shoulder, he turned, looking up, and saw the big policeman who had held him by the hair when they had searched the flat the previous weekend.

'Do you know, lads, how much that painting's worth, the one you pinched?' They sat, frozen in silent panic. 'Let me tell you who I am. I'm Robert Devonshire, I'm a detective sergeant. I'm looking for this painting and I can't find it.' He was speaking quietly, patiently, mockery edged with threat. 'Now look, lads, I know it's a bit late, but you could still say that it was a merry student prank. You could drop me a note, anonymous, you know, telling me where to find the painting. Left luggage for instance. Happy ending.' He saw that Charles was about to speak and cut him off. 'That's okay,' he said. 'Don't thank me.' He gave them a little wave, a beefy smile and walked out of the bar.

They looked at each other.

'How can he know?' said Les.

'Somebody saw us maybe,' said Charles. 'No, they can't have or he wouldn't mess about like this.'

'Just saw us hanging about, perhaps. Then they mention our names, get told what little sods we are. That could make us favourites, especially if they've no other runners.'

'It wasn't a good move, stopping to help Barney. A treacherous impulse to do good,' said Charles, smiling thinly.

'If they've not twigged it by now, they probably won't. Still, I'm not for going round to his house. Tomorrow, up at the university, I'll bump into him in the corridor and tell him he's in it. His face should be good for a laugh anyway.'

CHAPTER TEN

By the middle of the morning the coffee bar in Derwent College was beginning to be sordid; the tables marked with spilled coffee in dried rings and ashy puddles, the clutter of uncollected cups and saucers, of wet cigarette ends and biscuit wrappers. Les sat with his book perched on the end of the table. He tracked with his finger down the page as he read, his eyes flickering up from the print, absent from the conversation around him.

Then he saw Deborah. He felt a spasm of excitement and stared at her as she waited at the counter to be served, ready to catch her eye.

'You coming to Roger's seminar?' said the plump girl sitting next to him. She stood up and towered over him, provoking him and intimidating him as she always did. When he turned towards her his face was almost against her thigh, the thick flesh held tightly in her threadbare jeans. He stood up, abruptly, breathing in through clenched teeth, hissing softly with lust. The girl did not move and he had to stand tight against her as he rose.

'Course I am, Alice,' he said. 'He's good, Roger.' He touched the soft skin of her stomach, fingertips under her tee-shirt, hidden by her cotton jacket. He looked beyond the

59

girl, towards Deborah and there was Bernard Guy in his smart summer suit, bending and saying something into her ear. Les watched, stricken, as Barney laid his hand on Deborah's arm and she smiled at what he was saying to her. He turned away, horrified, staring at Alice, his hand on her hip.

'Bastard,' he said. 'Sorry, it's okay, just thought of something.' He took her hand and held it against his chest. 'Come on then,' and he walked out of the coffee bar with Alice, holding her hand, his heart pounding.

Two hours later Les stood at the foot of the concrete steps which led up to the biology block. The sunlight shone dizzily from the rough white walls. He made up his mind suddenly and bounced up the steps and on to the footbridge over the road.

He clattered down the narrow, over-clean corridors, peeking into open rooms. There were only the technicians and the odd, late student amongst the stale equipment in the large teaching laboratory.

'What time do you go for lunch here, then?' Les asked a grey-haired woman in a lab coat.

'The students went at a quarter past twelve,' she answered spitefully. 'If not earlier.'

'Dr Guy, where's his office?' Les was impatient, his eyes darting all around as he spoke.

'Well, he's gone off as well.'

'Right, great, thanks.'

He found them in Derwent College cafeteria.

He stood frozen, looking in at them through the enormous window. There was the loud splashing of the fountains from the water-court, two ducks walked away from him and dropped into the lake. He could see Barney talking away, waving his fork at Deborah.

'Dirty old bastard,' Les mumbled to himself. He banged on the window with the side of his fist. A flood of eyes flicked up at him and he blew a kiss at Deborah. She shrugged at him, her arms wide, asking what he wanted. He spread his body across the window, and hung there, arms outstretched, palms flat against the window. Deborah beckoned him with her spoon. He walked along the path, through the common room and into the cafeteria.

By the time he reached them they had finished eating. He put his tray on the table, sat down next to Deborah, leaning gently against her.

'You all right, love?' he asked her cheerfully. She looked at him blankly, perhaps hostile. 'Barney,' he went on, ignoring her coolness, 'we've got a big problem. But would you like the good news first?'

'Shut up. Not here.' Barney looked theatrically at Deborah, then, panicky as he saw the affront on her face, 'Les, be fair.'

'I've no secrets from Deborah, me,' said Les, maliciously.

'What's the matter, Barney?' asked Deborah. Les started to eat his curry. He put one hand under the table and held Deborah's thigh.

'It's us who thieved that painting,' he said conversationally. 'The cops know it's us and they're camping on the doorstep.'

'Oh no,' Barney almost whimpered, his heart crashed in his chest.

'No sweat,' said Les. 'Now, still on the bad news, it's all up to you Barney. You're emerging as the key man.'

'Oh, God, what now?'

'Good news: we can sell it. We think that we can find a

buyer, got some good addresses and all that. You, you've got to deliver, do all the leg work, make all the physical contacts.'

'Oh no.'

'Equal shares of between twenty, twenty-five grand. Look, you're up to your neck anyway.' Les finished his curry. 'Told you it was good news, didn't I?'

'Shut your mouth,' said Deborah. They both stared at her. 'You?' she said to Les. 'You and Barney?' incredulously.

'And Chas,' interrupted Les.

'Why do this in front of me?'

Les grinned at her. 'Hard to explain the real reason, but there is a subsidiary. You can take a message to Barney. You see him nearly every day when you're cutting up the rabbits and the rats and all that.' Her face was blank. 'One message, later on this week.'

'What's this real reason?' asked Barney. He was merely pale now.

'It's just too embarrassing, Barney. The message idea's good though, isn't it?'

'The real reason?' said Deborah. 'What sort of talk is that?'

Celia sat back against the wall of Deborah's room with the white sheet pulled up over her breasts. The sky outside was a soft purple dusk made darker by storm clouds.

'Lover?' said Deborah. 'No, not really. There's a man lurking around in that word.' She was sitting at the foot of the bed, drinking tea. 'That's why I like Les, I think. There are no burdens to carry with Les.'

'Les? Don't start liking Les.'

'I know, I know. He was licking his lips over some fat girl this morning.'

They fell silent. Finally Celia said, 'Well then, I'm off to the library for a couple of hours.'

'No, listen. Les came and found me having lunch with Barney. I could see he was pissed off, seeing Barney and I together. He told me that it was them, Charlie and Les, who stole the painting from Heslington Hall. Why tell me that?'

'He told you in front of Barney?'

'Barney's helping them to sell the thing.'

'It really was them? Oh fuck, they'll get crucified.' Then, indignant, 'Oh really. I can see Les doing this, but Charles does have more sense.'

'It looked true to me. Barney was terrified, Les was tormenting him of course. He said the police were on to them and, oh yes, he wanted me to be messenger between him and Barney.'

'You're going to take Les on, aren't you?' said Celia and Deborah nodded solemnly. 'You think that Les told you all this to keep you close to him; you think Les wants you.' Deborah nodded again. 'Is he devious enough to make you think that he wants you so that you'll be his messenger to Barney?'

'No,' said Deborah.

'No, he's not, is he?'

CHAPTER ELEVEN

Detective Sergeant Devonshire had had enough of these two clowns. He'd frightened them all right, but they were too smart to let the fear run away with them. Young Charles, though, might do a bit of good to hurt him; frightening was one thing, a good kick in the balls was quite another.

That tutor of his, mind you, he was a real beauty; emaciated, finicky little poofter.

'Charles Wilson? Oh yes, Sergeant, a wild unpleasant boy.'

Not being liked by that prat was a big mark in Wilson's favour. Dropped Wilson right in it. 'Family have disowned him, he has no money to live on from them, yet he lives so well, does he not? Such a lot of pilfering amongst the students. Seen around the Hall, was he? Well, the porters know their job, you know.'

Felt inclined to let him go to avoid pleasing the sod. Must get the painting, people were staying hysterical about it; bloody lords and vice chancellors and God knows what ringing up, collaring chief constables and politicians over the Tio Pepe.

He was sick of standing in this chip shop though. Gerry's few mid-evening customers were giving him funny looks. He could see the flat across the road and, at last, there was

Wilson. He waited until Wilson had turned to face the door, his hand going up to the Yale lock.

'Okay, Gerry, see you,' said Devonshire, slipped out of the shop and trotted across the road.

'Bastard,' mumbled Gerry and spat into the chip fat.

He timed it nicely. Just as Charles had the door swinging open, key out, he hit him, bundled him through the door into the dim hallway. Devonshire backheeled the door shut and went for Charles Wilson.

Charles had stumbled against the foot of the stairs, spilled the pile of books he had been carrying. He turned, half lying, to face Devonshire. Devonshire took hold of two great fistfuls of shirt and pulled Charles up. A crack of pain as Charles pushed as he pulled and rammed the top of his head into Devonshire's face. He hugged Charles to him and fell forward, his weight crushing Charles on to the stairs. Blood and tears pouring down his face, Charles pinned, squirming, underneath him.

Charles tried to get his knee into the big man's groin but the weight stopped him. He got a hand free and pulled hair, yanking the head back, feeling for an eye. Suddenly Devonshire was off him, pulled him up, crack into the wall and threw him down the hallway. He hit the closed front door side on. Devonshire was on him, hitting him twice, hard, low down in the belly. Charles fell over, retching.

Devonshire sat on the floor and felt his face. Charles was vomiting. Devonshire shouted, 'What a mess.' He looked at his hands covered in blood and mucus, rubbed them on his filthy shirt, wiped his eyes. He got up, got Charles up to his feet and pulled him, still doubled, up the stairs. He found the bathroom, let Charles fall on to the floor and looked at himself in the mirror. Swelling; one and a half black eyes in the morning he reckoned, nose gone again. He washed his face and cleaned himself with the towel. Charles was sitting up, pale and sick, watching him. Devonshire saw the eyes on him, poisonous, vindictive.

'This is going to be happening all the time now,' said Devonshire.

'You'd better watch your step, then,' said Charles.

'Painting,' said Devonshire, clubbing his fist on the top of Charles's head. Charles heard him going down the stairs.

At the hospital the doctor told him that he had a cracked rib. 'Football,' he said, 'more bloody sense you ought to have.' Welsh, more or less the same age as Charles. 'How did it happen, then?'

'I was crunched into the wallbars,' said Charles as he buttoned up his shirt. The doctor followed him through the door of the treatment room into the shiny waiting area of Casualty. They walked over to Les, who was waiting. Les saw them and pointed down the row of chairs. Twenty feet away sat Detective Sergeant Devonshire.

'It's a team-mate,' said Charles to the doctor. 'Same incident as a matter of fact. Lot at stake in these tournaments.'

The doctor went back to his room, returned looking at a piece of paper. 'Mr Devonshire?' he said inquiringly.

'We'll wait,' Les called as Devonshire was going through the door. He paused, but the doctor was close on his heels.

When the doctor had done with him Devonshire joined them at the coffee machine.

'Why haven't you made a complaint then? You so innocent. I'll tell you, you want to fade away from the spotlight, don't you? Well, no chance.'

'Why haven't you arrested Chas, then?' countered Les.

'Because you're right in it, aren't you, breaking into flats and thumping people?' He bent down and picked his beaker of coffee from the hatch in the machine. Devonshire put a coin in the slot and punched a button.

'Why not simply give it back? Nobody's going to get vindictive about this. Leave it on a table in the library, post it to the Bursar.'

'We don't have it,' said Charles.

'Now look, you've broken my nose you have. I'm being good, even bloody marvellous, about this . . .'

'You're wrong, you're just wrong,' Charles cut in.

Devonshire took a drink of his coffee. 'Nobody likes a smartarse, you know, Wilson.'

'Les,' said Charles desperately, 'tell him.'

'It's right, Sergeant,' said Les, 'we really haven't, you know, we haven't got it.'

Devonshire dropped his half-full cup into the cup that Les was holding so that coffee spilled over Les's hand on to the floor. He strode over to the door, flat-handed it open and walked away.

CHAPTER TWELVE

'Things have changed,' said Gordon and rubbed his distended stomach affectionately.

'Not that much,' said Roy Holland. 'There was always a market for specials, one-off stuff. You must know who'll take a nice picture like this one.'

'There might well be, but what's changed is that I don't know about it any more.' Gordon waved his short, fat arm in a half circle. 'See this shop? More a gallery, I like to think. Just a few good pieces, no junk littering the place up. Taxes paid, receipts signed. I've a bank manager, an accountant, a solicitor. What I'm not about to do is several years for the sake of a few thousand quid.'

'Gordon, give me a name. Stop the malarkey. I've got the message, I'll keep you right out of it.'

'Let's go for a drink,' said Gordon. Roy stood up and held out his hand to Gordon. Gordon grasped it and Roy pulled him upright. He was a great, fat man held solid and square by his worsted suit.

The pub was more or less a restaurant. They sat at a polished dining table, plain white plates in front of them, cocooned by polished mahogany dividers and etched glass. Gordon smiled up at the waitress as she served his steak and kidney pudding.

'Lovely,' he said, his bottom lip slackening to show wet, white teeth. 'Could you bring us two more Guinnesses? Lovely.'

'By God, Gordon, you're going to be like the Michelin Man.'

'Sod it, Roy. It's only a couple of times a week. White wine and lettuce usually. Not like you, you bony little bastard.'

'What about John Griffiths?' asked Roy. 'He used to buy and sell.'

'Dead.'

'Frankie?'

'He's a milkman last I heard. Love this pudding. Six, seven years ago that, mind.'

Roy sipped his Guinness, sat back and looked at the half eaten pudding on his plate. 'The over-the-hill mob, eh?'

'Finally, you understand. If I'm lucky I've got fifteen years left and I'm not spending them in Wandsworth.'

'Might as well burn the bloody thing.'

'Could do. Could show it to Lena as well though, couldn't you? Do you want a dessert? Crêpe, I'm going to have. They set 'em on fire, it's dead good.' He pointed at Roy. 'Never said a word, I didn't.'

'Why don't you come up home sometime?' said Roy, going back to his dinner. 'Susan would love it. Meet the grandkids.'

'Susan's a grandma? Well, even Northampton might be worth that sight.'

'You'll have to watch that with Susan. You start going on about that and she'll smack you one, no problem.' Roy put some kidney into his mouth, broddled around on his plate. 'Lena's got a number, has she?'

Gordon looked at him and sighed. 'You don't half bloody come it. Look in the phone book.'

★ ★ ★

Lena's house in Wimbledon was huge. Roy took a tube and arrived at its gate with the A to Z still open in his hand.

He wasn't ready for Lena. Her skin was a dull amber and clung to her bones. Her face was hollow, the bone at her temples jutting.

'Ah,' she said in false sympathy, 'bit of a shock, is it?' She turned her back on him to walk before him into the house, he couldn't see any shape under the long caftan she wore. The blue was just right for her black hair, but she was fleshless under it. She sat him down in a sofa with loose covers patterned with big roses. He stared at her, stricken, shocked out of tact.

'Right,' she said. 'Let's get the obvious out of the way to start with. I'm dying. Coming up very soon.'

Roy stared and stared. He remembered plotting desperately to get Lena into bed; her flesh under his hands. The tears welled up.

'Oh, fuck off, Roy, if you're going to start that game.'

'Sorry, Lena, I'm sorry.'

'Not seen him since nineteen-eighty odd and what does he say? "Sorry". What happened to "Hello, nice to see you, give us a kiss"?' She sat down beside him and took his hand. 'Stay and have some dinner with me. Still love me a bit then?'

'Oh, I do, I do. I'd not realised.'

'Nice to be loved.' She smiled at him and he could see her teeth, enormous in the sore, sticky gums. His heart lurched.

He didn't want his dinner, but he sat and ate it for her. She sat him down at the kitchen table and watched him eat.

'What do you want?' she said. So he told her about his son and Charles Wilson and their painting.

'To be honest,' he said, 'I'm scrounging around for a way to

71

get rid of the thing. Get them off the hook.'

'Give it back,' said Lena.

'Would you?'

'What is it?'

'Portrait by Wyndham Lewis.'

'The York one?'

'That's right.'

'Should be okay. Collectable. Or we could sell it back to the insurers.'

'Just like that?'

'Course not just like that. Might take months. That's the problem, Roy, I've not really got months.'

'Best look sharp then,' he said, near to tears again.

'What we should do,' said Lena, 'is get a move on so that these silly young buggers of yours are clear and free.' She went to a kitchen cupboard and took out a bottle of cognac and a glass. Roy could smell the heavy spirit as she poured it. 'That will mean that they'll have to accept a low price and I can pass it on quick to someone who can afford to wait.'

'How low?' He said it lightly, without any thought that she might be cheating him.

'Seven thousand maybe.' She gave him a tight smile, her own eyes now bright and fragile. 'There's not much point in my making anything on it.'

Roy sipped his cognac. 'Lena.' She looked at him, head on one side, sarcastic. 'What're you doing here on your own?'

She spread her hands in a resigned shrug. 'Why not? Got to be somewhere.'

'It's nice,' said Roy hesitantly, apologising, 'but it's a bit bleak. I mean, it's so big.'

'Only at night, Roy. It's a nice house. There's a big conservatory and the garden's lovely.'

'Garden, you?'

'Come on,' she said, 'I'll show you.'

She beckoned him out of the kitchen. He followed her into the hall and into a dim room, an office with desk, filing cabinet, cream plastic keyboard and display screen. There were double doors at the end of the room, glass, beaded with dark wood. Lena took him through the doors and he could see the sky through the arched glass roof. The plants were pressed closely, tight shadows, sharp razor shapes of leaves.

'Just a second and I'll get the garden lit up,' said Lena. He was going to stop her so that he could continue staring out at the night, but the garden sprang up at him, white light shadowing and blurring the flowers and bushes. They stood looking through the window. Lena took his hand and felt him stand closer to her.

'I think the lads are getting into trouble with this, Lena,' he said. 'Help me get them out of it.'

'Is he like you, your Les?'

'I don't know. Susan says so. He's a scruff, mind.'

'You were never that.'

'He wears suits. He wears one non-stop until you have to chuck it away; cut it off him nearly. Tee-shirt and pumps he has on with it.'

'Is he clever?'

'Clever? Bloody right he is. They wanted him to go to Cambridge at school. I had a right go at him when he wouldn't. Called me a snob; arriviste. I went and looked it up.' He laughed at her. 'Then I went back and cracked him one.'

'Shall I meet him?'

'After. When we're all in the clear,' he said, thinking that "after" might be a bit late.

'Come on, Roy, I'll drive you to the station. Euston, isn't it?'

'I'll tell you the arrangements the lads have made; very sensible they've been. They've roped in a messenger.'

The train whizzed him through the grimy night, flicked the back ends of small towns across his eyes.

Lena's old flat on Putney Bridge Road and Lena, twenty-five years old, sumptuous, pouring for him the first wine that he had ever drunk, giving him dinner at night, Lena's arms, her shoulders, freckles gliding over her flesh.

CHAPTER THIRTEEN

They were sitting on the top deck of a bus, coming back from the university.

'You see her, then?' said Les.

'That's right,' said Deborah. 'And Celia says that Charles can go and fuck himself.'

'And not her.'

'Correct.'

'And I've to tell him?'

'No, you're not to pass on any messages at playtime. What you have to do is simply keep your big wet nose out of it.'

Les was hurt and looked away, his bottom lip pushed forward. He rubbed at the window with his fingertips and peered out at the street.

'Our stop after this next one,' he said. Deborah put her arm through his.

'You'll fall over that lip,' she said. The bus threw them against each other as it roared slowly around the narrow streets. 'If we get off here we can walk round the walls.'

They got on to the city wall where a steep lawn banked up against it. There were flower beds, brash summer flowers. They began to walk along the white stones towards Micklegate, stopped to lean and look over at the railway station.

'Who's the fat girl?' Deborah asked.

'Where?'

'No, clown. The fat girl you spend afternoons with.'

'Fat girl?' asked Les, offended. 'I don't like fat girls.'

'You like this one well enough to fuck her in the afternoons.'

'Fat? Alice isn't fat.' He shook his finger in her face stumbling. 'I don't like fat.'

'Dump the bitch,' she said, staring fixedly away from him at the taxis creeping away from the station.

'If you say fuck once more,' said Les, 'I'm going to smack you in the mouth.'

'You're not getting into bed with me if you're getting into bed with other people as well.'

'Look at people when you're speaking to them.' Les was shouting and when she twitched her head round her face was white. 'You're right, I agree' – still shouting at her.

'Good,' she said, pushed herself upright, away from the wall and walked away.

Les walked behind her. After a couple of minutes he put his hand on her shoulder and was walking with her. He could feel the softness where her shoulder rounded and gripped her tightly as they walked, more slowly, in the afternoon sun.

Just before Micklegate they climbed down steep, stone steps to the pavement.

'Oh no, it's him again,' said Les. He stopped at the last step so that Deborah was blocked behind him 'What's up?' she said.

'Look.' He pointed and she went back a step to see over his head. A large white police car was parked by the flat door. It was on double yellow lines and its blue light was flashing. Devonshire was leaning against the car, looking at their front door.

'Waiting for Charlie, are you?' said Les, pulling out his key. Devonshire was right up behind him, waiting to push inside.

'Excuse me,' said Deborah. 'Is this your car?'

'What?' Devonshire looked over his shoulder towards her.

'That's a double yellow line you've left it on.'

'What,' said Devonshire, screwing up his face, 'what's that?'

'Double yellow line. The police are subject to traffic regulations you know as well as . . .'

He heard the door slam. Les Holland was gone, Deborah put out her tongue, stuck up two fingers at him and ran back to the steps, on to the wall and away.

'Of course we can expect him to keep on trying us out,' said Charles Wilson. 'What else can he do?'

'It's a right pain in the arse,' said Les Holland. 'We could send the thing back, Charlie. It's not really a lot of money, is it? I mean, we'll only get a tiny percentage of what it's worth.'

'No chance, he's the sort to come and gloat.'

'So what?'

'So it's nice as well to drop the university in it.'

'Don't be stupid,' said Les, beating his fist on the table so that beer slopped over the rims of their glasses and his fist made splashes. 'You can't drop things like universities in anything. Universities aren't even things, I don't think they're even concepts, they're . . .'

'Oh, shut up.'

'Why don't we go and do a bit of arson? That would upset the university, wouldn't it? That would make it sorry for itself, we could go and kick it on its walls and call it names. People are the things you can get at, Chas.'

Charles folded his arms and stared down at the table. 'Has

your father fixed us up or not, then?' he said.

'He has, yes.'

Charles sat up straight. 'Well, what's all this give it back nonsense, Les? Come on, get Barney on the road. Action. Let's get going.'

'If we get pinched,' said Les, softly, 'what will you say?'

'What about?'

'If we get pinched with the money or the picture or whatever, how do you plan on explaining how we came to have made the contacts. Contacts with Dad's old contacts?'

'I thought,' said Charles, unpleasant and sarcastic, 'that I'd drop you and your dad right in it. You know, I'd tell the police how you'd led me astray, made me do these things against my better judgement. You bastard.'

'Look, don't come all that how-could-you-think-it-of-me crap. Think something good up.'

'Edited highlights of the truth would do it, I should have thought.'

'Go on.'

'Pointless to deny knowing you and Roy. So, I should say that I met people socially through your father and cultivated them on my own without his knowledge.'

'Right then,' said Les, reluctantly, 'better get Barney off and running. And that's not going to be easy. Big, flabby rabbit, he is.'

'Did you tell Celia?' asked Les.

'What about?' said Deborah. Les heaved at the corkscrew and slopped wine on the kitchen floor as the cork jerked out.

'The painting.' He poured two glasses half full. 'And Barney and Charlie, all that.'

'No,' said Deborah, 'not a word.'

'Well?'

'Well what?'

'What do you think?'

'Nothing.'

'Nothing? What do you mean?'

'I mean, do whatever you like, I don't know anything about this sort of thing, I haven't got an opinion.'

'What if I get caught?' protested Les, indignant.

'Tough shit.' She stirred the spaghetti sauce and turned the gas right down. 'About twenty minutes,' she said.

'Yeah, sure,' said Les. He walked out of the kitchen, across the hall and into his room. He sat at the table and began writing, forcing his mind into the technicality of his essay, nursing his hurt feelings.

'Good, is it?' asked Deborah. She came into the room, sat on the bed drinking her wine. Les kept his back to her, pretending to work, feeling his heart bump.

'Yes.'

'I'm surprised you bother.' She drained her glass and lay back, turned on her stomach and rummaged through Les's cassettes.

'Use the headphones,' said Les.

'Why do you bother?'

'I'd like a first, two one would do.'

'You, what for?'

'For a career.' He carried on writing. He heard Deborah clicking around with the tape deck and then George Formby clattered out at him: 'Mr Woo's a Window Cleaner Now.' He put his pen down and spoke angrily through the cheerful voice, 'I'm very clever; I am, you know. I'm better than most people here and my essays are better than most of the books that I read and I like doing this. So that you being a suburban shit . . .' He turned round, ready for a good shout. Deborah was naked. Sitting cross-legged in the middle of the bed, she smiled at him, bounced up and down, singing.

'Bloody hell,' said Les.

'Not now, Deborah. I've booked time at the computer centre.'

'Here.' She held out a white envelope at arm's length, waved it under his nose.

'What's that?' He looked furtively down the row of workbenches but the students were paying him no attention, bent over microscopes, computer terminals, candied rats. Deborah slid the envelope into the pocket of his lab coat.

'That's me finished. If it needs a reply, find somebody else.' She walked back to the rat's eye that she had been slicing.

In his cubicle in the computer centre Bernard Guy ripped open the envelope:

Dear Barney,
When you have read this letter burn it and eat the ashes.
*   Take the stolen painting to 12 Victoria Avenue, Wimbledon, on Saturday afternoon. You are expected.*

*   Yours in crime,*
*   A. Friend.*

He went and sat on the lavatory. He flushed away the bits of the letter, sat down again and put his head in his hands.

Bernard Guy was shocked when he saw the woman who opened the door. Her skin and yellow eyes silenced him.

'Come in, dear,' she said. Her voice was confident, soothing. Barney walked past her into the soft light of the hallway. 'I'll take that, shall I?' she said and picked the suitcase out of his hand. 'Go into there,' she said, pointing to the room which led into the conservatory. 'You'll find the drinks table in amongst the ferns.'

Barney opened a door. 'This one?' he asked.

'That's right, dear, won't be a minute.'

Barney did as she told him and was pouring tonic into his gin when he heard her again.

'Not for me,' she said, smiling, and Barney flinched as he saw her long teeth and raw gums.

'Nice plants,' he said.

'They were here when I moved in. The gardener sees to them.'

'Part of my field, plants.'

'Well, they would be,' said Lena, thinking him odd. 'Most fields have them, I suppose.'

'What?'

'Plants, in fields.'

'Oh no,' said Barney quickly. 'My field, it's biology.'

'Silly,' she laughed, 'of course, that's right, you're from the university as well.'

'No,' said Barney, 'I'm not from anywhere. Look, I'm not normally rude, but I'm going to go.'

At the front door he turned and said, 'Get somebody in to catalogue those plants. You've got some good stuff there.'

She stayed in his mind, as the tube train rattled him through the sunlight towards King's Cross, that yellow emaciated woman. 'Dear', she had called him. Her voice had been soft. In the racket of the station bar he had a few drinks and forgot about her.

Lena sat amongst the plants looking at the summer sky through the glass. It was warm and still and, as the night drew in, the foliage turned into shadow and then to darkness.

CHAPTER FOURTEEN

'I've been to Northampton before,' said Deborah. 'We went to a shoe factory. Earls Barton, I think it was.'

The train was crawling towards Castle Station. There were signal boxes, a wide mesh of tracks and then the station closing quickly upon them. The instant of silence as the train stopped, a clatter of doors, shuffling and then the platform. Les looked around for the exit sign.

'There we are,' said Deborah, pointing to stairs which went up to a footbridge. He stopped her as she tried to walk away.

'Look,' he said, 'I'm a bit nervous about this.'

'Never.'

'Don't be clever, Deborah. It's a bit deliberate, is this. I mean, when I was at home girls came round . . .'

'A lot?'

'Stacks. But I feel a bit stupid about this.'

'Thanks.'

'I feel as though I'm bringing someone home for Sunday tea, as if I'm doing something formal, declaring myself.'

'So, declare yourself.'

The train pulled away and left them feeling alone in the wide space it left. They walked over the footbridge, struggled to find their tickets and were out into the sunlight.

'Is that heavy?' said Les, pointing at Deborah's shoulder bag.

'No, I've only got a nightie.'

'We'll walk up to the bus station then.'

They sat upstairs on the bus and she could see the bland newness of the town-centre shops, glimpses of an older town and then the jumble of small shops, pubs, restaurants.

'Wellingborough Road,' Les told her. 'Best bit of town.'

The green of a clipped park opened up on their right. She saw inside its gates a wedding group, posing for photographs. Les got up and rang the bell. 'Come on, then, Mummy's been simply dying to meet you.'

Les went in through the kitchen door; his mother was on her knees, her head in the oven.

'Deborah,' he said, 'I'd like to introduce you to my mother.'

Susan Holland backed out of the oven. 'Hello,' she said. She got up and kissed Les, holding her pink-gloved hands away from him. 'Oven cleaner,' she explained and went to the sink, pulled at the gloves and dropped them into the bowl. She turned and smiled at Deborah. 'Hello, duck. Come on and sit down. Bring your bag or Mick'll chew it.'

'Mick's the dog,' Les explained. They both gave him a look. 'I'll make some tea, should I?'

When he carried the tray through into the sitting room Deborah and his mother were standing looking out of the window.

'Make sure you do, then,' his mother was saying.

'Do what?' asked Les.

'Have a proper career and not let some man screw it up,' said his mother.

'And have you anyone in mind who might be about to screw it up for Deborah?'

'Nobody much.'

★   ★   ★

Les was watching cricket on the television when his father came home. He was lying on the settee cuddling Mick and drinking beer from a can.

'Hello, son,' said Roy.

Les twisted his head round and said, 'Hello, Dad.'

'On your own?'

'Apart from Mick.'

'What're you doing?'

'Sulking.'

'Where are they then, your mother and thingy?'

'Gone down town.'

'Hit it off, have they?'

'They're a bloody pair, they are.'

'That's all right, then.'

Roy Holland pulled the dog off the settee and shooed it out of the room and into the kitchen. It slunk under the table, turning its back on him. He went back into the sitting room, knocked Les's feet off the cushions and sat down.

'What's the score?' he said, nodding at the screen.

'Dunno.'

Roy put his arm around Les. 'Go and comb your hair and we'll go for a pint before tea.'

'Dinner.'

'How do you mean?'

Les got up and took a comb from his back pocket. He ducked into the mirror. 'I've a feeling we'll be having dinner tonight.'

The walk to the pub cheered Les up. It was a warm, gentle evening, the gardens and the trees were heavy and green and over the road there were still people in the park. Mick walked along with them, past the cricket ground and led them in through the doors of the lounge bar.

'Evening, Mick,' said the barman. The dog sat down on the carpet and barked.

'Billy,' said Roy Holland.

'Now then, Roy, Les. What can I get you?'

He put the pint glasses in front of them, walked round the bar and put a clean ashtray full of beer in front of Mick. 'Drunken bugger, this dog is, aren't you, love?' he said, rubbing the dog's ears. There were two groups of men waiting at the bar now and he bustled back. 'Right then, lads?'

Roy and Les took their drinks and sat in the bay window where the light filtered through red and green glass.

'You've not had words, have you?' asked Roy.

'No, it's all right,' said Les. 'We've not heard about the painting, Dad. What do you think?'

'It'll be a long job. You'll be safe with Lena, though.'

'It'd be nice to have some spend for the holidays.'

'Prat, you can't spend it.'

'I was going to go abroad and spend it. You know, go off somewhere on a cheap student fare and then switch to a spot of luxury where no one can see.'

'Yeah, well, maybe then. I've heard nothing. Your Charlie, he's the one to hear. He's the name.'

'Bit protective, eh?' said Les sharply.

'That's right.'

'Look, Dad,' said Les awkwardly, 'could you ring up? You know, ring Lena and ask how it's going?'

'You don't want much.' They sat in silence, Les not wanting to pester. 'Can't do any harm, I suppose,' said Roy. 'We can stop at the box on the way back.'

Les stood outside the box with Mick. He watched his father dial, listen, put the phone down.

'Answering machine,' said Roy. 'It said she'd be unavailable for some time.' He paused. 'Don't people do answering machines in their own voices? Wasn't Lena's voice, that.'

'What do you reckon?'

'Don't know. I'll ring Gordon up, he'll know.' He took Mick's lead from Les and walked off, preoccupied.

'Come on,' said Les. 'What's up?'

'Lena, well, she was really ill. You know, dying, I suppose.'

'What about the picture?' Les began.

'Bugger your picture,' said his father quietly.

When they got back to the house Susan was in the kitchen, cooking.

'Deborah's in the bath,' she said. 'Hello, love,' and she kissed her husband.

'I've to phone Gordon,' said Roy.

'Ask him when he's coming up,' said Susan.

Gordon told him.

'Lena's in the hospital,' he said, 'in Putney. I can't see her coming out, to tell you the truth, Roy.'

'Have you seen her?'

'Well, I went in, but she's not conscious.'

They talked about Lena and when they were young. They both said how lovely she had been and talked about being in bed with her.

Roy went into the lounge and sat on the settee at Les's side.

'What's up, Dad?' said Les. 'You all right?' He looked at his father anxiously and saw he was crying. 'Don't worry about the painting at least. We only nicked it anyway.'

Les had never seen his father in tears, it shocked him. A part of the world crumbled. It was as if a sudden ageing had robbed his father of the strength to climb the stairs and he, Les, was the one looked to for competence and order; he held his father's hand. Roy Holland blew his nose, wiped his face and gave a heavy sigh, blowing himself empty of breath.

'I'll go and have a word with your mother.'

Les watched him out of the room and then could hear his parents' voices in the kitchen. He left the room himself and went upstairs. He hoped that Deborah had not locked the bathroom door.

CHAPTER FIFTEEN

Charles Wilson stood on his own at the college bar. He had been working all day in the library. Saturday night had taken him by surprise. He still had the feeling of isolation that working in the stillness of the vast library gave him and was glad to stand quietly in the dark, noisy bar. He drank his beer and watched the two barmaids serving drinks, chattering and laughing with the students. He liked the one with dyed yellow hair and tried to catch her eye, smile at her, but she flitted off, pulling beer pumps, clattering money into the till. She was leaning over the bar, saying something to Celia. Celia smiled at the barmaid, put her bag on the bar and rummaged in it for money. He stood back from the bar, out of the light so that Celia might not see him, and stared at her. The dress she wore was very pale, her arms were brown and he could imagine the fine hair on her skin.

He pushed his way through to her; she was putting change into her bag. He put his hand on her arm, could feel the skin, the muscle, soft, tensile. She was not startled at his touch, but when she turned and saw him the smile fell from her face. She stared at him and said, 'I'm with someone else.' The words came out sharply. Charles looked at his hand on her arm and then back at her face. He stared at her; she made no move away from him. Finally he took his hand from her.

'Well then,' he said and looked away, walked back to his corner of the bar. When he picked up his glass he looked across through the lights of the bar; Celia was still there. She saw him looking at her, picked up her tray of drinks and turned away.

Charles finished his beer and shouted across the bar to the barmaid with yellow hair. 'Pint, please, when you've a minute.' She came over to him. In her thirties he guessed as she smiled at him, showing a mouthful of crooked teeth.

'Bitter, is it, love?' she asked. He nodded and she started to fill his glass. 'Girlfriend is she?'

'It doesn't look like it.' When he offered her the money she took his hand, briefly, stroked it.

'Ah,' she said, 'poor thing.'

'Don't mock. I'm crying inside.'

'I can see.'

He leaned on the bar, his weight on his forearms. Someone's shoulder bumped against his and he looked to his right and saw the big, shaven-headed boy with whom he had often seen Celia. They stared sideways at each other.

'James, isn't it?' said Charles.

'Celia's upset,' said James. Charles still stared. 'If she should be upset by you again,' he went on, but Charles interrupted him.

'Fuck off, you bald bastard.' James took hold of Charles by his shirt front so that he could feel the knuckles biting into his chest. Charles hit him once, hard, on the nose with his beer mug. There was blood and beer everywhere. Glasses smashed. There were shouts and cries as James flailed about. Charles walked out of the bar, he paused at the porters' lodge. 'There's a terrible scene in the bar,' he shouted and the porter came out of his office.

'What's up?'

'In the bar,' said Charles as he stepped through the door into the night. 'There's a skinhead in there causing trouble.'

Les Holland sat with his mother in a corner of the public bar. Chuck Berry was on the juke box. It was smoky, hot and crowded. Across the room Deborah was playing darts with Roy and two of his friends.

'Who is Lena, then?' Les asked.

'She was a girl your dad lived with in London,' said his mother. 'He's very soft you know, your dad,' she added quietly.

'Did you know her?'

'Course I did.'

'Oh.' Les sipped his drink and looked away, across the room to his father and Deborah. 'In London, like?'

'No, love. She came to see us up here a time or two. She was nice. I liked her.' She turned to face Les squarely. 'Who's put a poker up your arse then?'

'You what?'

'We weren't born married, you know, Les. Lena was somebody your dad was in love with, still is, it seems, and I like him the more for it. If you ever manage to grow up, so will you.'

'Okay.'

'Well, bloody hell.'

'Sorry.'

Les and his mother sat, quietly angry with each other. Les could see his father's friends eyeing up Deborah. His mother followed his stare.

91

'Do you like this one then?'

'How do you mean?'

'I've missed the girls more than I've missed you, I think.'

'What girls?'

'All those poor little buggers who used to trail round after you. Me and your dad used to worry that you were taking too much on.' She smiled maliciously. 'You know, that you were living beyond your means like.'

'Mother.'

'Anyway, it's nice to have one about the house again. Mind, she's a sight more about her than your others.'

'I like her a lot actually, Mum.' His tone stopped her. She held his hand.

'Well, just you be a bit gentle with your father, love.'

Charles walked for half an hour before he was able to wave down a taxi. The walk had calmed him and he sat brooding over Celia. He got out of the taxi outside King's Manor. The old building was lit and he could see that the doors were still open. The porter looked out at him as he passed the lodge.

'I'm locking up soon.'

'I'll not be long,' said Charles mildly. He could sense the hostility as he walked up the stairs. The common room was softly lit and empty. Charles sat in one of the big, blue chairs and closed his eyes. 'This is no good,' he thought.

He passed the porters' lodge again on his way out. 'You can lock the door now, you miserable sod,' he shouted.

The Black Dog was more like it with the crashing din of the juke box, edging into violence; rat-faced Alfie braying at the bar, the creamy fat landlady downing gin and screaming at the dope smokers sitting under the darts board; tinsely, tattooed wives drinking snowballs, fat breasts under Marks and Spencer sequins.

Charles stood at the bar with Alfie admiring his Brylcreemed hair slicked back from greying side burns.

'Safe went down the stairs,' said Alfie, 'and him, silly bugger, keeps hold of the rope.'

Out in the street at half past eleven he turned down Alfie's offer of fish and chips and walked off on his own, away from the city wall, towards Celia's flat. He stood on the pavement opposite, the railway cutting black behind him, and looked up at the dark window.

Les lay, in pyjamas, under his duvet. The settee wasn't quite long enough and he thought that he would put the cushions on the floor when the film finished. Deborah was sleeping in his bed. He lay thinking about his father being in love, his mother's delicacy, her lightness. He turned off the television and remade his bed on the floor.

Mick's head lifted when Les switched on the light in the kitchen. He pulled the dog into the lounge and they lay side by side under the duvet and went to sleep.

CHAPTER SIXTEEN

They sat opposite each other over the tiny restaurant table. It was warm and gloomy. Les Holland was eating lemon meringue pie.

'What sticks in my bloody throat is that they are going to get it back,' said Charles Wilson.

'But won't it be entertaining telling Barney there's no money for him.' Les thought for a moment and added, 'Imagine if he's left his fingerprints on it.'

'Don't be silly.'

'He won't think it's silly. He'll shit himself.'

Charles stacked their dirty plates and pushed them to one side. He leaned over the table looking as though he were trying to weigh Les up.

'What?' said Les.

'Lena.'

'Yes?' Les leaned forward so that their faces were inches apart. 'This is a plot coming up, isn't it?'

'Is she actually dead?' asked Charles, ignoring the mockery.

'She's in hospital.'

'And because your father heard only an answerphone her house must be empty.'

Les sat back in his chair. 'No chance,' he said, 'not me.'

Alan Smith

'Listen, it can't be difficult, can it, breaking into houses? People do it all the time.'

'Not me, I don't break into houses all the time. Me, I'd be worried about locks and burglar alarms. I'd be worried about not knowing where to look in a five, six bedroom house.'

'What we'll do,' said Charles, 'is hire a car for a few days, zoom down and have a look at the place.'

He looked up, half startled, and then smiled at the waitress, 'Oh yes, thanks,' he said to her. 'All finished, hang on we'll pay you now.' She told him how much she wanted and he pushed the notes into her hand. 'No, don't bother with the bill,' he told her. She stood, confused, with the money in her hand. 'Is that enough?' He offered her another five pound note.

'No, that's fine,' she said, reassuring him, apologising.

They pushed past her and out into the narrow street.

'You're on your own, pal,' said Les.

'Now, Les, let me buy you a drink and explain why we must do this.' Charles put his arm round Les's shoulders, speaking airily, but Les stopped him. 'No, I'm not rummaging round in houses belonging to my dad's friends. I'm not putting Dad at risk to join in some piece of obscure psychological vengeance that you've cooked up.' He stood away from Charles, leaving his friend's arm raised in the empty shape of embrace. 'It'd be simpler, if it's just giving the painting back you can't put up with, simpler to burn the fucking house down, wouldn't it?'

Charles Wilson's face lost its anger and he smiled a sickly, mocking smile.

'Oh shit, no, come on, Charlie,' said Les Holland.

They parked across the road from Lena's house. Les lay as far back as the front seat of the car would allow.

'We can't stay long, Charlie, the curtains will be twitching.'

'It's a nice big house,' said Charles. 'Take a fair bit of looking through. I'll have a look round, I reckon.'

'No you bloody won't,' said Les. 'You go wandering off round here and you've got to have a good reason. Suburbs, this is, pal. They sit around yearning for burglary, well, house-breaking as it's daylight. Get it into your skull that this is a maximum security zone.'

'What then?'

'Let's change a wheel.'

'Very amusing.'

'Cover, isn't it?' Les sprang the seat upright and rapped on the dashboard with his fingertips. 'Come on, drive. Let's take a look around the neighbourhood. Get to know the streets, tube stations, dead ends, all that.'

Charles drove carefully through the tree-lined streets, past the high hedges and sober, family houses. He turned in to a pub car park. They walked through smart, revolving doors into a half-panelled hallway. Double glass doors led into a sombre lounge bar furnished with heavy armchairs and polished mahogany tables. They took their beer from a waistcoated barman and sat down at the edge of the room.

'If it was in and out,' said Charles, 'no problem.'

'Yes, I know. I said all this before we hired a car and drove two hundred miles.'

'If we could just know where she put it, then we could be in, grab and off before the cops arrived.'

'You admit there'll be alarms then?'

'The big yellow box I saw on the house wall, the one with alarm written on it, suggests that there might be,' said Charles. 'Where would you hide a picture?'

97

'Don't know,' said Les, woodenly.

They watched the room filling up with men and women in suits.

'Fancy that myself,' said Les, looking over at the lasagne the man on the table next to them was eating. He waved at the waitress. She ignored him.

'Keep waving,' said Charles.

'Professionals probably have hidey holes for stuff like that; not like us, just sticking it on the wall,' said Les. He stopped waving. 'Mind you . . .' Charles was looking at him, smiling.

'How did Barney deliver it?'

'Don't know.'

'Did he simply bring it down in its frame?'

'Don't know.'

'Did she simply hang it on the wall?'

'Don't know.'

'What was the picture he put it behind?'

'He never said.'

Charles sat looking at Les and Les knew what he wanted.

'Now, don't tell me no, Les, listen first. The two of us go in, one upstairs, one down. Just a few minutes in the house; a quarter, a half minute in each room. We go in, put the lights on, look around the walls and if we don't see Barney's picture, well, we don't.'

It was too much for Les. 'I think that you make Barney less angry than I do, Chas; you'd better ring him up.'

There was a phone booth in the hallway of the pub, a mahogany cupboard smelling faintly of sweat and lavender. Charlie rang Directory Enquiries for Barney's number, rang it but there was no reply. He tried the university and found Barney in his office.

'Bernard? Charles here, I've been trying to get you.'

98

'Not on the phone,' said Barney and rang off. Charlie went back to Les.

'He won't speak on the phone.'

'What did you say?'

'Hello, Bernard.'

Les was laughing, 'Come on, then,' he said, 'back up the M1.'

CHAPTER SEVENTEEN

It was late that afternoon when they rang Barney's doorbell.

'Barney,' said Charles and smiled at him when he opened the door, 'there's good news and there's bad news.'

Bernard Guy went white at the sight of them. 'Go away,' he said and then, as anger replaced fear, 'fuck off, go on, fuck off.'

'Can we come in?' asked Les.

'We can't stay long of course,' said Charles. 'The London train goes in about an hour.' They showed no sign of being ready to go; Barney looked at them suspiciously, breathing more heavily as his temper mounted. He turned aside and they brushed past him into the house.

'Any chance of a coffee, Barney?' asked Les.

'Be my guest, feel free, help yourself, fait comme fucking chez toi.'

'Could do with some sandwiches, Barney,' said Les, cheerily. Barney walked out of the kitchen and into his lounge. He sat in one of the armchairs, hand to mouth.

'Don't do this Bernard,' said Charles from the doorway. Barney looked up at him, but before he could speak Charles said, 'He and I drove to London this morning to weigh up the prospects of a spot of burglary that we shall have to do.'

'No, not me,' said Barney, 'not another word. I'm not in this, not me.' He beat his fist on the arm of the chair. 'Have a cup of coffee, have a sandwich and then go away.'

'We can't sell the painting any more so you aren't going to get a thousand pounds. The police or someone like them are about to find the picture, with your fingerprints on it, I suspect, and put two and two together.'

'Coffee,' said Les from behind Charles. They both came into the room and stood looking down at Barney. 'Oh, sorry, Barney, did you want one?' He saw Barney's face. 'Christ, what's up?'

'Sorry, Les, I told him. I think he did leave his fingerprints on it.'

'Well, what a trick, Chas. You knew I wanted to tell him.' He turned to Barney. 'Did you, though, Barney,' he asked with blandly false concern, 'put your fingers all over it? Put yourself right in it you have.'

'It's a good job that we might be able to help you,' said Charles.

Bernard Guy stared at Charles. 'Where is it?' he said. 'What have you done? I gave it to that woman.' He pointed his finger, accusing, almost petulant. 'I did my bit and I didn't cock it up. What have you done?'

'Well,' said Les, 'to be serious.' Barney looked at him cautiously, then at Charles, questioning. 'No, really, Barney, serious. Look, the woman in Wimbledon, she was a nice person.' Les was awkward, not wanting to give anything to Barney, but unable either to make fun of him with anything to do with Lena. Barney caught his seriousness and paused in being angry and afraid.

'Yes, she was. I was only with her a few minutes, but she was nice.'

'She's in the hospital, Barney, and she's dying. We don't know what she's done with our picture.'

Barney rushed for safety. 'Ditch it then, let someone find it. They'll give it back. Cut our losses.'

'Fingerprints, Barney,' said Charles.

'Bollocks,' said Barney. 'I haven't got a record and once they've got it back they won't give a damn anyway.'

'Which picture frame did you put it in, Barney?'

'The Andrew Wyeth, Old Boot, why?'

'The poster?'

'That's right. The one that was in the hallway. So what? It's lost now.'

'The one in the plain Habitat frame, wasn't it?' said Charles. 'You took it down and handed it over in its frame?'

'In a suitcase,' said Barney. 'I gave her the suitcase, she went off with it, upstairs I think. Never even gave me the case back.' Barney squared up to them. 'Now, that's the end for me. Nothing else. No more. Go away.'

'Can we use your phone, Barney?' Les asked.

'I suppose so.'

While Les was looking through the book, dialling, listening to the ringing, Charles sat with Barney.

'No thousand pounds then, Barney?'

'What are you going to do?'

'In or out?' He saw Barney hesitate, calm down. 'Lot of money, a thousand pounds.'

'There's a train in twenty minutes,' said Les. 'Come on, leave Barney alone, get your skates on.'

'See you later,' said Charles. 'Oh, don't pout, you silly old sod. I'm only taking the piss.'

Bernard Guy turned on the television set. Laurel and Hardy.

★ ★ ★

Charles leaned on the formica-topped table. 'Les,' he said, 'one last effort at this and then we'll let go.' The train shuddered and hauled itself out of Doncaster station and the twilit countryside opened up around them. He tried again. 'Five minutes, in and out. A quick look round and if it's not there then up and away and forget it.'

'We should have kept the car,' said Les.

'No, you need a stolen one for something like this.'

'Do you know how to nick one?'

'No. You?'

'No.'

'What then?'

Les leaned forward, putting his mouth close to Charles's ear. 'It makes things more difficult. We'll have to get something to carry it in.'

'We could roll it up and put it in a cardboard tube. We could buy a poster, shops stay open late in London.'

'Okay, we'll use the underground then. The station's not far from Lena's.'

'It's masterly.'

'Every detail.'

CHAPTER EIGHTEEN

Once they were inside the garden gate the high hedge concealed them. Its shadows from the street lights ended about ten yards short of the house. They squatted down and looked at the dark building in front of them.

'It would be better if we could get round the back,' said Charles. 'I'll go and look. If I'm not back in a couple of minutes, I'll be at the side there waiting for you. Don't run.' He stood and sauntered up the drive, drifted across the front of the house and vanished into the shadows. Les counted to a hundred, couldn't bear to be still, walked briskly after Charles. He walked across the front of the house and into the sudden, absolute blackness between the side of the house and the tall conifer hedge. He jumped when Charles took hold of him.

'Piece of piss,' said Charles softly.

It was dark, too, in the back garden; all around it were the black, shadowy masses of hedges, shrubs, trees. They were standing on a paved area decorated here and there with tubs of flowers. The great, high prow of the conservatory butted out from the house, the glass flat and textureless in the darkness.

Les was frightened. He was frightened of the house, black

and empty, its passive spaces waiting to swallow them. Charles's face was up against his, pale with violence.

'No, Chas. Come on. Let's get out of it.'

'You what?' Charles was hissing. 'Five minutes, you fucker.' His face thrust into Les's so that Les felt the stubble on his friend's cheek and beneath it the soft flesh against his own. Charles turned from him and walked towards the double doors of the conservatory. He bent and picked up a large, angular stone from the rough edge between the flagstones and a flower bed. 'You do downstairs,' he said. 'A quick look in each room, with the lights on, then off to the tube and we'll find each other on the next train back.'

He turned his back on Les and smashed three panes of glass, top, middle, bottom. Les cringed at the noise, saw him fiddling with bolts and lock. Charles faded away from him into the obscurity of the house.

Then it wasn't dark. Charles was switching on lights as he went through the house, irregularly, as he chanced on switches. Les followed him at the run. Conservatory then an office, bare walls. A hallway, three doors. There were mirrors in the hallway, cupboards in the kitchen, a calendar. Dining room and lounge had switches inside their doors. Dutch domestic scenes in the lounge, fruit and a nude in the dining room.

Les, crying out softly with haste and fear, stumbling back through the conservatory. Pitch now after the lights. Guessing at the direction of danger he ran down the back garden until he reached the clutter of canes and cold frames, the turned earth of the vegetable patch. He pushed his way through the hedge, a thin screen of lilac, and over the low brick wall into another garden. The back of this house was dark. He ran towards it. There were lights and he could see into a kitchen. He veered off to his right and crouched under the hedge, ten yards or so from the corner of the house. The door opened and a fat, old man in a cardigan stood emptying a kitchen bin into the bin outside. As soon as the door closed behind the man, Les ran down the path at the side of the house. The gate was high and closed. His fingers scratched over the rough wood, found the bolt. He stopped himself, breathed, slid the bolt, shut the gate behind him. The line of the hedge sheltered him to the front of the garden and he was through the front gate on to the bare pavement.

Across the road was the pub where they had been that afternoon, its lights spilled over the shiny cars and gaudy inn sign. Les walked past it to the underground station. 'Get off the street,' he thought.

It was the response time that did for Charles Wilson. There was no alarm he had thought. No bells nor electronic whooping to panic him. The Wyeth poster was leaning against the wall under the window of the first bedroom he looked into. He changed his mind about rolling the painting and carrying it off in the cardboard tube, worried about damaging it. He looked in the wardrobe, sliding the mirror doors which covered a whole wall. There was a small suitcase on the floor. It was empty and he put the painting, frame, covering poster, new-bought cardboard tube and all into it. 'Bit of a triumph really,' he said to himself, grinning at his own cockiness.

He turned off the light and looked through the window at the placid, sodium-lit street. Then the pale car pulled up outside. Fear swamped him as the policemen hurried up the drive towards the front door.

The back bedroom looked out over the glass roof of the conservatory. Out of the window he could lower himself on to the narrow ridge of mortar where the line of the conservatory met the house wall. He could edge down the pitch of the conservatory roof spreading himself against the house side. After the guttering it was only seven or eight feet to the ground.

He pushed the suitcase under the bed, finished with it. The sash window stuck then banged up with a clatter. He looked down into the garden, watching for the policeman's torch. Nothing. Backwards out of the window, searching with his foot for the ridge. Finding it. Both feet on the ridge and then more and more again of his weight. He pushed his body outwards, fingers and toes he remembered from rock climbing at school, so that he could look down and place his feet. His right foot edged down the slope of masonry which stood proud from the wall before the timber frames began. The ridge sagged under his left foot and destroyed his balance. The weight of his body sank through his left leg as he sought equilibrium. The ridge moved again, then there was nothing beneath him. He fell backwards through the glass.

CHAPTER NINETEEN

Les Holland sat on the lawn at the edge of the lake that wandered around the university.

'You're a shit,' said Celia. 'You and him, a pair of shits.'

'I've not seen him, love, honestly. I saw him when Deborah and me got back from Northampton. I went for a meal with him and I've not seen him since. Not for, what, two days now?'

'You've been off somewhere, the two of you.'

'I've not. I've been working.'

'Where?' she asked scornfully.

'Up here at the library, King's Manor, at the flat.'

'I couldn't find you.'

'I like to dodge around, you know that.'

Celia stretched out her bare legs and shuffled nearer to the lake's edge so that she could dip her feet in the water. She winced at the cold.

'They know it was him, everyone saw him. He broke James's nose. He had to go to the hospital.' Les said nothing. He lay on his side, opened his book and began to read. Celia persisted. 'They'll throw him out.'

'No, they won't.'

'Of course they will, you fool. That tutor of his can't wait to get rid of him.' Les rolled on to his back, put the book up to shade the sun from his eyes.

'Tell James,' he said, 'to deny that it was Chas.'

'Why should he do that?'

'Tell him that if Chas gets the boot that it will be his, James's, fault and that he'll always have it on his conscience. Tell him that if he denies it was Chas then he, James, will feel like a truly wonderful human being. If that doesn't work, offer to fuck his brains out.'

'I do that anyway,' she said coldly. Les caught his breath.

'Threaten to stop then,' he said coldly back.

She stood up and looked down at him. 'I'll tell him that Deborah's going to stop fucking him as well, shall I?' She stayed frozen above him, horrified at her own words. Les tilted the book so that he could look at her. 'It's not true,' she said. 'I said it because I was mad.'

He ignored her.

'You and James lie about it. It doesn't matter if the lies are obvious, just keep on lying and nobody will want the hassle. Will he do it, this James lad?'

'Of course he will,' she said, miserably.

'Then,' Les explained, 'he can break Chas's nose when he sees him next.'

Les was sitting at the desk in his room. He was reading, making notes with a heavy black pencil in the book's margins. When the doorbell rang it startled him and he sat back, blank for some seconds. It rang again. He went to the kitchen and looked through the window, down into the street. Deborah was standing by the door. She didn't look up. As soon as he opened the door she said, 'Where've you been?'

'James,' he said and pointed a finger in her face, touching her nose almost. She swiped his hand away.

'That's right,' she said, flying into anger. 'Since the night you pissed off from the dance and ditched me to go stealing paintings.'

'Well stop it,' he shouted and hit her, flat-handed, across the head.

'I have,' she shouted back and hit at his face with her bag. It was heavy and his cheek was bleeding. People were stopping to watch them, curiosity beating their unease.

'Stop crying,' said Deborah, desperately. She pushed Les through the doorway and slammed the door behind them.

He walked up the stairs in front of her, went into his room, sat down at his desk. When she came into the room he turned round in his chair and said, accusingly, 'All that crap you gave me about my fat girl in the afternoon, about not sleeping with me if I'm sleeping with somebody else.'

'Well, I knew about that,' she said. She was shouting back. She raised her bag above her head and threw it with all her might down on to the bed.

'Oh, right then, sorry, I'd misunderstood. Deceit, hypocrisy, lying your bloody head off, that's all fine.'

'Of course it is, you wingeing, sentimental, working-class twat.'

'I loved you.'

'Past tense.'

'Past tense. Piss off.'

'No.'

Les stood up, knocked the chair away and turned to face her. She met the turn of his head with her right fist. She caught him over the left eye and opened up the skin so that the blood ran and he couldn't see. It was suddenly red all over his face and down his neck. He stepped back and fell over the upturned chair.

Deborah looked down at him. Les didn't offer to get up, didn't wipe the blood, stared at her, one-eyed and bloody.

'Everybody lies all the time to everybody else,' she said, 'about love and sex and lust and how they feel.'

'Silly cow,' said Les.

'They do.'

'They don't.'

'Do.'

'Help me up.'

'You'll get blood all over me.'

'Didn't ask to be hit.'

He got himself away from the chair and sat up on the floor his head hanging so that globs of blood fell intermittently on to the carpet.

'I bet this'll need stitching.'

'I've hurt my hand,' said Deborah.

'Where?'

'Can't move these fingers.'

'Go and put your hand in a bowl of cold water. I'll ring for a taxi.'

CHAPTER TWENTY

It was twilight when they got back from the hospital. Deborah's hand was strapped, two of her fingers were taped together. Les had an oblong gauze pad taped over his eye, the eyelid was yellow and blue and swollen and closed.

When they opened the street door they could hear voices in the flat above them. They looked up the stairs and Charles Wilson's personal tutor was looking down at them. Les ran up the stairs, pushed past Frank Vernon and looked into the kitchen. There was a thin woman with black, curly hair.

'Who's she?' said Les, pointing at her.

'Miss Wilby works in the registrar's office,' said Frank Vernon. His voice was high, always on the edge of strain. It suited him; he was a tall, thin man with a big, bony-looking head.

'Well, get out of it the pair of you.'

'Wouldn't it be an idea to ask why we are here?' Smug, sarcastic.

'All right then.'

Vernon almost spoke but Deborah came into the kitchen and he stopped and looked at her.

'Go on,' said Les, more belligerent.

'Your friend,' said Vernon slowly, unpleasantly, 'has been identified at the scene of a crime.' He paused, smiling, waiting for Les's reaction.

'Which friend?'

'Wilson, Charles Wilson. He's in the hospital, Putney, I think. He won't be coming back here because I should think that he will be going to prison.'

'You,' said Les, 'piss off.' He jerked his thumb towards the stairs.

'When we've packed his things,' began Vernon but then Les was on him, pushing his bruised, half closed face forward, good eye popping with rage. Les walked into him, pushing him with his shoulder and chest until he was at the top of the stairs.

'Very well,' said Vernon, almost forgetting himself and tossing his head in indignation. From halfway down the stairs he called back, 'You can't put this off. I shall be back, you know.'

'I'm sorry about this, missis,' said Les to the black-haired woman.

'Stop shouting, Les,' said Deborah. Les leaned on the door jamb, breathing heavily.

'Sorry,' he said again. 'Sorry, I've forgotten your name.'

'Catherine Wilby,' said the woman quietly.

'Sit down,' said Deborah to Catherine Wilby. 'You too, Les.' Les stayed in the doorway looking at the two of them as they sat at the kitchen table. 'Will you tell us what has happened?' said Deborah.

'Mr Wilson, Charles, he was found in a house near Wimbledon Common two nights ago. By the police.'

'Why is he in hospital?' asked Deborah.

'He didn't try and fight them did he?' Les Holland's voice

was going up again. 'The bloody clown, I'll bet he did.'

'No, he didn't,' said Catherine Wilby. She looked at Les, sorry rather than awkward. 'He'd had a fall, you see, through a glass roof. The police were very good, as a matter of fact, they were careful not to move him. He fell through a glass roof affair you see.' She stopped, lost in the words.

'Go on then,' said Les.

'He's conscious now, they said that on the phone, but they're not letting him move until they're sure what it is that he's damaged. He can't move anyway, though.' She sat silent.

'Is he paralysed?' asked Les, astonished, afraid.

'Yes, he is.'

'What? How much?' demanded Les. Catherine Wilby gestured shakily towards her neck.

'Below here, they think.' She faltered then added, 'It's not sure.'

Les pushed himself up from the door jamb, turned and walked into his room. He shut the door behind him.

'Give him five minutes,' said Deborah. 'What packing is it you want to do?'

'Personal things to start with.' They were whispering to each other, their heads nodding closer together. 'Then, eventually, the rest of his stuff.'

Robert Devonshire watched Frank Vernon leave and waited for Catherine Wilby. He saw her put a suitcase into the boot of her car and drive away.

The street was pale in the evening sunshine. He crossed Micklegate and rang the bell. The window banged open above his head and he saw Les looking down at him.

'What do you want?'

'Let me in.'

Les pulled his head back into the flat and stood looking at Deborah.

'Might as well,' she said. Les went back to the window.

'Oi,' he shouted and, as Devonshire looked up, 'catch,' and threw down the front door key.

The three of them sat round the kitchen table and Devonshire said, 'I can't let go of this. I'm sorry about your mate, but I can't let go.'

'I've told you before,' said Les, 'I've not got this painting of yours.'

'It's not mine, Les,' said Devonshire. 'It belongs to a bloke called Wayne Barker, Barker's Media Systems. He's a right shit, he is. Now, you give back the painting or you'll be joining your pal Charlie.' He stood up to go. 'If I'm truthful I reckon you'll be joining him anyway. Be careful, Les. At least try and keep yourself out of it.' He stood up and looked down glumly at the two of them.

They heard him go down the stairs and bang the door.

'Was he threatening?' asked Les.

CHAPTER TWENTY-ONE

Charles Wilson looked up into his friend's eyes. Les Holland's face was very close to his.

'Stale beer,' said Charles. 'Where's the suit? It was just getting a nice shine.'

'Deborah,' said Les and stood back, arms outstretched, to show himself off. 'Clean clothes.'

'I like the shirt.'

'I made her steal it. Very masterful I was. "Steal the shirt or the suit stays." Not sure how she did it, mind; don't they have electric tags?'

'Bet she bought it.'

'At least she lied.'

'Even better then.'

Les sat down in the hospital armchair and looked across at his friend. Charles lay in starched white sheets. His face was already tight.

'When you cry,' he said, 'and you're lying like this, on your back, you can't get rid of the tears. They gather in big pools over your eyes.'

'Don't cry then.'

'Well,' said Charles, 'I've been frightened.'

Alan Smith

'What's wrong with you anyway, Chas? What do they reckon you've done?'

'There's a young guy, about our age, one of the doctors, he's been coming in and talking to me. I quite like him, actually. He reckons that I was lucky. If I'd landed on my head and crunched the top end of my spine, I'd have paralysed myself from the neck down.'

'The shitbag. He shouldn't tell you things like that.'

'No, no, that's been the best bit so far. A very dramatic moment: fear and panic, claustrophobia. Then I calmed down. Felt very good about that, being able to calm down. Proud of myself. Then he told me that eventually I'd be able to limp around and not to get dramatic. I can't move now, but with the plaster off and once I heal up inside, well, limping should be on the cards.'

'Don't cry,' said Les. He wiped Charles's eyes.

'Clumsy bastard,' said Charles. 'Shock, you see. It makes me have a little cry every now and then.'

Les leaned back in the chair again and looked around the room. There were bottles suspended from frames over Charles's bed; tubes vanished in the sheets. The walls were bare and drab.

'How long will you be here for?'

'Not long.'

'Then what?'

'Then nothing.'

'What happened, anyway, at the house?'

'Found the painting quite quickly. I put it in a suitcase. That's under the bed in the back bedroom if you're interested. The cops arrived so I went out by the back window. The conservatory roof collapsed and here we are.'

'What's going to happen?' asked Les, hopelessly.

'Nothing's going to happen.' Charles was matter of fact but then he slipped into a bitter harangue. 'It's boring; even when catastrophe still has a bit of novelty to it, it's boring. It's going to get more boring. Things are going to happen to me and I won't be in the action, I'll be at the far end of it. Just before it comes to a halt. Everything stops here.'

'Stop whining,' said Les.

'That's psychology, is it?'

'No, that's me getting sick of you.'

'If you come really close, Les, I reckon I could just about manage to nut you.'

Les stared at him glumly. He thought about the police and the trial and whatever there would be after that. He thought about Robert Devonshire and his warning about Wayne Barker.

'Have you had an erection?' Les was suddenly bright.

'Lots.'

'No, fool, since you've been in here.'

'No.'

'Oh, well.' Les sat back again, worried now for what he had said.

'Mind you, Les, there's not been cause, scope or provocation.'

'Try it then.'

'You don't excite me, Les.'

'Look, I'll go and ask the doctor.' Les was on his feet.

'Don't be crude, Les.'

'Come on,' said Les. 'I'll have to ask him straight. I mean this could be your salvation, a real interest. If he says it might be on I'll go and get some dirty books and we can have a trial run.'

'We?'

'Then I can ferry in some live ones. They'll be queuing up, man.'

'What if I get Aids?'

'Well, you've no future anyway.'

'That's okay then.'

Deborah was waiting outside. She was sitting on a bench which looked out across a small green on to the front of the hospital. Les came out of the hospital and crossed the road to join her. When he was still some way from her she stood up and when he reached her and she could see his face wet with tears, she put her arms round him. He put his hands on her hips and held her away, kissed her.

'Come on,' he said and, holding her hand, pulled her along for the first few steps until she gained her balance and asked:

'What's wrong with him?'

'Like they said, he can't move.'

'At all?'

'He can blink, swallow, stuff like that. Oh yeah, he can breathe on his own.'

She stopped walking and jerked Les to a halt. 'For ever?' she asked, appalled.

'No, for God's sake.' He hung his head. 'But he's broken up, legs, ribs, God knows what else. And he's had an operation; things punctured, burst.'

Deborah waited for him to move but he stood, hopeless with misery. She put her hand on his shoulder and pushed him into a walk. When he was moving she put her arm round him and they went awkwardly down the street.

She stopped at the first pub they came to and sat him down. She bought him tomato juice and a plateful of food; lasagne, chips, green beans.

'Eat,' she said.

'No, not now.'

'Eat. For shock. Fill yourself up, it absorbs the shock.'

'What about you?'

'I'll have some of yours,' she said and put a bean into her mouth then two chips. Les ate his way through the pile of food.

' Beer would be good; it's a bit stodgy all this.'

When she came back with his beer he had finished eating. 'You're right, it slows you down all that. How did you know?'

'My mum told me.'

'Funny thing for your mum to know. Jogging and T.S. Eliot I'd have thought.'

'Don't' – warningly.

'Oh, come on; over forty, suburban intellectual, Clive James and brown bread.'

'You're all right, then?' Deborah looked at him sarcastically. He looked back, suddenly ashamed.

'Yes.'

'Tell me about Charlie, what's going to happen to him?'

'One of two things he reckons. He could stay where he is or he could go to a private place. Of course, there's always the trial to look forward to. I never knew how rich he was. He's been telling me. I can't understand it, Deborah. We've spent nearly all this year thieving. I mean, why thieving? We could have burnt things down, vandalised, taken the piss, done all sorts. But no, Charlie always wanted to go thieving.'

'Don't ask me. Anyway, you did all the other things as well, didn't you?'

'Burning?'

'Question of time.'

'Well, it could have been on, but it's my dad, see; he's finished it for me.'

'You didn't tell him?'

'Only about the painting. It wasn't stopping me like that anyway. It was seeing him in love with this Lena years and years on and my mum telling me off for being small about it. Put me off conflict a bit that's all.'

'Tell me how rich Charlie is.'

'Rich family in all directions; big country house, flat in Westminster. Millions and millions and millions, Charlie says.' Les took a drink of his beer. 'Not that he'll have anything to do with them, hates his mother and father.'

'He's got no option.'

'How do you mean?'

'Look, they'll come along and cart him off if they want to.'

'They bloody well won't, you know.' Les was suddenly angry, as suddenly quiet. 'Could they?'

'Course they could.'

'He can refuse. He's not a cabbage you know. He's still intelligent, assertive. He can read, talk, all that.' And then Les brightened. 'Oh yes,' he added dramatically, 'and erections.'

'Erections?' Deborah was astonished, then shocked. 'You bastard, what have you been talking about with him?'

'It's fine, don't worry. Came to me like a flash of light.' He saw her looking at him tight-lipped. 'Honest. He said he was bored and we talked about it and we reckoned it'd be an interest for him.'

'An interest? You're a halfwit,' she shouted at him. 'Are you going to trot a string of whores into the hospital?'

'Quiet,' Les hissed and they looked round at the room of faces turned towards them. 'It'll be friends, won't it?'

'Like me?' she asked belligerently.

'No.' He was hurt. 'I thought we could kick off with Celia, then my fat girl, perhaps.'

'They won't do it. You're a fool.'

'I thought that at first, but then I reckoned that they'd feel guilty, mean, saying no and that I could work on that, all that guilt. Then when they'd done it once, it would be easy, well, relatively easy, to keep it going.' She was intrigued and leaned over to him.

'Seriously?'

'Don't you think?'

'It's immoral.'

'No, stupid. Nasty things are immoral. This is a nice thing we'll be doing. Generosity, affection, tenderness, joy, therapy. We couldn't be doing a better thing.'

CHAPTER TWENTY-TWO

'Darling,' said Charles Wilson's mother. He looked silently back at her. 'You simply cannot carry on with this pose; all this being angry. Whatever your motives or your purposes you simply must face the reality that it is to your family that you must turn now, not some ridiculous, undergraduate friendship.'

She bent to open her handbag, which was on Charles's bed, and took out cigarettes. Charles watched her light one and inhale the smoke.

'Don't smoke in here. I don't like the smell. It's bad for me.' She looked at him, irritated. There was nowhere to stub out the cigarette. 'Put it in the sink,' said Charles. 'And then you might open the window, to let out the smell, you know.'

His mother pushed at the over-painted window, banged it with the flat of her hand before it would open. She stayed by the window so that she was in a part of the room that her son could not see. 'You ought to come home,' she said. He did not reply. 'We could create whatever facilities you need, hire staff.'

'You want to look after me, Mother?'

'There ought to be specialist staff for that.'

'You don't want to look after me, Mother?'

She stared at the window, saying nothing. Charles went on, briskly, 'Get the lawyers cracking then. Get the money free from all those covenants and conditions and whatever. Use mine. Get the house kitted up; a self-contained bit, I don't want to see you or Father when you're there.'

He fixed his eyes on the ceiling, not staring but looking somewhere away from her as he heard her walk from the window.

'I have to go,' she said. 'May I kiss you?'

'No.'

'Who was your visitor?' said the nurse later on that afternoon.

'Tall, slim, black hair?'

'Yes, that's the one.'

'That was my mother.'

'She went to speak to the doctor.' She was pulling and straightening his bed. 'Bet you'll be away soon,' she said.

'Why do you say that?'

'Oh, come on now.' She was annoyed. 'With all your loot you're not going to stay in one poky room.'

'You're Irish.'

'Course I am.'

'Sorry, I'd not noticed before.'

'Why should you?' she said, angry, hands on hips.

'What's the matter with you?'

'Never mind.'

'Find out what Mother wanted with the doctor, will you?'

'Why, yes, course, straight away, young Master Charles.' Charles stared at her. 'Well?' she said.

'Can't do it.'

'What?'

'Shrug. I'm trying to shrug my shoulders and I can't do it.'

'I'll count you as having given me a good shrugging, shall I?'

'Dream on.'

'You or me,' she said. Charles looked at her. She had black hair and her skin was white. 'Don't stare.'

'I'll stare if I want to. How old are you?'

'Twenty.'

'I'm twenty-one,' he said. 'Shit, do my eyes for me, will you?'

'What?'

'My eyes, dammit. When I cry I can't get rid of the tears.'

'Don't cry then.' She wiped his eyes.

'I keep doing it; shock, the doctor said. Gently, they're eyes, not somebody's bum you're wiping.' And suddenly he was reminded of Les.

'Get stuffed,' said Celia. 'That's disgusting. It's disgusting.'

'He's ill, for God's sake,' said Les desperately. 'He's broken up.'

'Dying?'

'There are tubes going into him, you bitch.'

'Dying? Of course he's not. They're going to patch him up. He'll be all right.'

'He's on his own; it'll be months.'

'Do him good, the bastard.'

'You don't mean it,' said Les.

'A good teacher, your friend,' said Celia.

The fat girl looked at him, amazed.

'No,' she said. 'How could you?' She sat down next to the pool table and cried.

Alan Smith

★ ★ ★

'Told you,' said Deborah. 'It's a half-witted idea.'

'You agreed.'

'Only because I'm spending too much time with you.'

'What?'

'What do you mean, "agreed"?' she asked sharply. 'You want me to, I suppose, do you?'

'No,' said Les, half shouting.

'Well then,' said Deborah.

'How can you hold the phone?' asked Les.

'This nurse here, she's holding it for me. Now, listen, Les, tell me, when's the funeral?'

'What funeral?'

'Lena's funeral.'

'Assuming she's dead?'

'Ideally.'

'I don't know when the funeral is,' said Les bitterly. 'I'll find out, shall I?' finishing at a shout.

'Sorry, Les. Don't get upset. It just struck me that if Roy was going and you went with him, you could pop upstairs and pick up the picture.'

The line hummed between them. Charles waited until, finally, Les said, 'Your nurse, you've told her all about this, have you?'

'Bits.'

'Oh, good.'

'There's no need for that.' There was more emptiness on the line. 'One more thing. That bastard Vernon, he's written to my mother.'

'What for?'

'To tell her that I'm going to be chucked out.'

128

'Good old Frank. I'll bet he enjoyed that.'

'I've not gone yet, Les.'

'About this nurse?'

'We're in love. Her name's Eileen.'

'You're what?'

'Never mind.' Charles was laughing. 'How did you get on with Celia and all the other girls?'

'You're in love.'

'You went ahead and put it to them?' asked Charles, amazed.

'I did.'

'And they'll be along shortly?'

'Well, I've time if I rush. I'll tell them you're in love, that should stop them.'

'Are you serious?'

'They were moved.' Les tried to get some wistful sincerity into his voice.

'Er, well, look.'

'No, you being in love and she being your nurse, it's best to cancel.'

'You bastard, they all turned you down.'

'Turned you down, actually.'

'That's okay then. As long as you don't feel hurt.'

'What about this funeral business, Chas. Are you serious?'

'It would tidy things up. If they found the thing in the house of your father's friend, me, your friend, having been captured burgling the place, they can't fail to make some sort of a connection. I mean, no matter what I say.'

'Yeah, I know. I've been a bit worried about that.'

'Anyway if you get the damned thing we could have a bit of fun with it.'

CHAPTER TWENTY-THREE

Roy Holland didn't want to drive in London. Les had come down from York and they would travel down together on the train.

In the early evening he walked with his father and Mick down to the pub. The landlord went into his routine, serving the dog first and then pulling pints of bitter for them.

'All right, Les?' he asked.

'What? Oh yes,' said Les.

'What about you, Roy?'

'Sorry, Billy,' said Roy Holland. 'Don't take any notice. We're burying a friend of mine tomorrow.'

'Oh, I see.'

They took their beer and sat at a table by the wall farthest from the bar. They watched Mick slurping his beer up from the big, white ashtray. Billy came round the bar, split a packet of crisps and put it down by the dog's head.

'Greedy bugger,' he said to Mick. He looked up at Roy and Les. 'A few crisps'll not hurt him. I've given him them organic crisps, sea salt and cider vinegar. Do him good.'

'I don't want him spoiled, Billy,' said Roy. 'You'll have him vegetarian next, going jogging, watching his fibre.'

'It'll make him fart,' said Les.

'He's a good dog, that,' said Billy defensively.

'Bugger the dog, Billy,' said a man at the bar. 'Come and serve.' Billy went.

'It's not right you know, Les.'

'Dad, it's not a bad thing. It's only sensible.'

'I'm not very keen on sensible right now. Anyway, I told you sensible weeks ago. Very bloody sensible; falling through a roof, being had up for burglary.'

'I know.' Les looked into his glass, subdued.

'I suppose you're right, mind,' said his father.

Les went to bed after the nine o'clock news and sat up, reading. It was a couple of hours before he heard his mother and father come up the stairs to their room. There was toing and froing and the murmur of voices until almost midnight. Les sat there in the silent house; he would have felt better with Mick in bed with him but the dog was too frightened of Les's mother to come upstairs.

He couldn't get Robert Devonshire out of his head. Devonshire's concern worried Les. The notion that he might be due to join Charlie frightened him. He went to the window and looked out over Abington Park, dead under the flat light of the street lamps.

Eric Ellis sat outside in his hired Ford Escort and waited until the last light went out. He told himself that if he were back at six there shouldn't be a problem.

Back at his hotel he telephoned Wayne Barker.

'No,' he said, 'I'm sure I'm right. There's only the Holland boy on the loose, I'll follow him.'

'Now listen, Eric, don't go frightening this lad; grab him when you know he's got the picture. I don't want any police. Get me my picture quietly so no one knows.'

'What about Holland?'

'Shut him up.'

Eric Ellis lay in bed thinking of ways to shut Les Holland up. He knew what he wouldn't do, anyway.

He slept until five and at seven he saw Les, his mother and father drive away from their house. He followed them to Castle Station and saw them go to the platform for the London train.

Ellis bought a ticket for London and waited a little way down the platform from the three of them. When the train came in he found a seat in the same carriage as Les and Roy, several seats away. Susan left while the train was still standing at the station. The three men sat reading newspapers and the train bumped into motion.

In London Les and Roy went into the underground; Ellis followed them. They reached Wimbledon at about half past ten.

Outside Wimbledon Station a tall, fat man was standing by a black Ford Granada. When he saw Roy Holland he raised his hand in greeting.

'Roy,' he shouted and as Roy reached him he put his arms around him.

'Now then, George, thanks for meeting us.'

'That's all right, Roy.' He nodded at Les. 'This the lad?'

Ellis watched Les shake hands with George. He stood by the kerb and waved at a taxi. It U-turned across the traffic and pulled up in front of him. He got in and said to the driver, 'Wait here a minute. When that black Granada starts off I'd like you to follow it.'

Les sat in the back of the Granada and listened to his father and George.

'It's all been delayed,' said George. 'What with her living

133

on her own, no relatives. It was the solicitor got in touch with me and I got in touch with some of her friends and so on.'

'Is there going to be a crowd?' asked Roy.

'Well, yes, there is as it happens. People thought a lot of Lena. I mean, she hid herself away these last few months, but before that she got around.'

'She was always a bugger.'

Les watched his father and George grin at each other.

'We were like little savages to her, me and your dad,' said George.

'Noble, though,' said Roy. He turned round to look at his son. Les looked away from his father and watched the street flick past. He wasn't feeling good about pushing himself and Charlie into his father's old affair. Now, his father and George being so gentle with each other, delicate and mischievous, as they thought back to Lena, made him guilty.

They had to park some way from Lena's house because of all the cars.

'I've had some caterers come and put on some snacks,' said George. 'There'll be a drink for us before we set off. Lots of it. I told them. I mean, she liked a good piss-up, didn't she?' George stood in the front garden, tears rolling down his fat old face. Roy held his hand.

'You can stop this bloody game,' he said sharply. 'Come on, George.'

The house was full of people; middle-aged people, old people standing quietly.

Les stood with his father, rode with him in George's car to the church and cemetery and back to the house.

They were all much more cheerful, the burden lifted and gone. There was a lot of drink and Les watched his father as if he were suddenly a stranger, unreal, amongst people from a past which pre-dated his mother and Les himself.

He left them to it and went out into the hall and up the staircase. Outside the window of the small back bedroom, the roof of the conservatory was roughly covered with heavy-duty builder's polythene. He took off his jacket and shirt and laid them on the bed. Beneath the bed he found Barney's old suitcase and in it the Wyeth poster. The metal clips which held the glass in place were stiff and, fumbling in his nervousness, he wrenched back his fingernail. The pain of it stopped him and he looked at the finger as blood darkened under the nail and oozed out. He went more slowly, though his heart screamed at him.

The painting was still there. From his jacket pocket he took a large polythene bag and put the painting flat inside it. He took from another pocket a roll of surgical tape and stuck three long strips across the length of the polythene-covered painting. Kneeling up on the floor he held the painting to his torso and stuck it to his skin with the overhanging ends of the tape. To make sure he used more lengths of tape to make the painting fast to himself. When he had put back on his shirt and jacket, fastened his black tie, he reassembled the poster in its frame, put it back in the case and under the bed.

Feeling stiff and awkward he went back downstairs to what was now a party. His father was sitting on the settee with fat George; they both had glasses of whisky. They were looking into each other's eyes and singing. 'Norwegian Wood' – a girl they had both had.

They were singing quietly, George crying, his father laughing, taking hold of George's hand. No one, apart from Les, paid them any attention. There was a lull in the noise of the room and their voices carried loudly turning heads towards them and Les saw suddenly his father at the centre of the world as he had been all through Les's childhood. And then, as suddenly, the strangeness vanished and he felt the polythene, moist and clinging on his skin.

Les made them leave George's car and take a taxi.

'Because you're pissed, the pair of you,' he said, sternly. They left George outside a vast Victorian house in Putney and went to the station.

Ellis lost them when they took the taxi from Lena's house. He went straight to Euston and waited, hoping. He saw them leaving the taxi. Les was carrying a plastic bag but Ellis couldn't imagine that he had a painting stuffed in that. He found a seat well away from them, amazed that they had not noticed him.

'How are you feeling, Dad?'

'Not too clever, Les, tell you the truth.'

'Here you are,' said Les and put a bottle of Perrier on the table. 'Drink that, it'll clear your insides up.'

'Boy wonder.' Roy drank nearly half the bottle. 'I think I'll have a little sleep. Oh, by the way, everything all right?'

'But of course.'

'Boy wonder,' said Roy and closed his eyes.

Les sat up and watched television with his parents. The painting was upstairs between sheets of stiff cardboard, wrapped in brown paper. Les was wondering who to send it to.

'Sod it,' he thought. 'There's no rush.'

Outside again Eric Ellis was tired and hungry. He risked a walk to the telephone box near to Roy Holland's local.

'Devonshire?' he said.

'Speaking,' said Robert Devonshire. 'Who's that?'

'Eric Ellis here, Sergeant. I'd like a little help from you.' There was silence. 'It's very simple and if you prefer it you can regard this as information received and all that crap, okay?'

'Go on, then,' said Devonshire reluctantly.

CHAPTER TWENTY-FOUR

'At the moment,' said Celia, 'I think it's disgusting, all of it.' They were sitting facing each other across a table on the top floor of the big, white library.

'Don't be so prim,' said Deborah gently. 'I never supposed that you were spiteful.'

'Not a terribly pleasant thing to say.' Celia looked down at her book, dismissive.

'There's no pleasant involved in it,' said Deborah. 'Descriptive not normative.' She pushed the books forward across the table so that they dug into Celia's breast. 'These silly buggers that you read all day go in for that sort of talk, don't they?'

'It's horrid,' said Celia, 'blurting out bits of sexual gossip, like some damned girl in Woolworths. I can tell you why, too. It's because I'm jealous of Charlie and envious of you.'

'Jealous and envious, what, I say,' said Deborah, sniggering. 'Tough shit that.'

'Should I go and see Charlie?' said Celia suddenly.

'No,' said Deborah. 'I wish that when he fell through that roof that he'd landed on his neck. He is, and there's no doubt, a complete shit. Stick with good old James.'

'He's a bit dull.'

'Not very. Think of his hidden assets.'

'Well, I do. I think about them all the time,' said Celia wistfully.

'Put that crap away and let's get out of here.'

'No,' said Celia, 'another hour or so and then the library shuts anyway.'

'I'll see you then, in the bar over in Derwent.'

Deborah walked down the wide, central staircase and out into the mild, summer night. The white walls were softly lit under a blue-black sky. She took the footbridge over the road and went into the jumble of buildings with the lake opening out beyond them to her right. She looked back at the library towering behind her and to its right the biology laboratories; there were still lights there. There were always people there checking and fiddling with experiments.

To fill the time before Celia would free herself of the library and because, too, she liked the laboratories, liked the slow, patient confidence that went into the work, she retraced her steps over the road and went into the dry, zoo smell of the biology block.

Bernard Guy's door was open but when she looked in, the office was empty. The big teaching laboratory was more like a workshop; lines of benches with sinks and retorts, jumbles of tools and overalls. Barney, at the far end by the wall, was sitting on a table, his back to her, staring at a workbench. Her footsteps made him turn.

'What are you doing here?' he said.

'Saw the lights, wondered who could still be working.'

'All the other things I like doing cost money,' he said mournfully. 'Anyway, I like doing this more than anything else.'

'Is it yours?' Deborah asked him, gesturing at the experiment.

'No, it's Brian Jackson's. He thinks it's looking like a waste of time, but he's wrong.'

He started to tell her about the experiment, gabbling at first as he tried to find a starting point for her, but then speaking more for himself, slowly, mulling over the ideas and possibilities. She sat on the bench watching him, seeing the discipline, the half ironic style that kept enthusiasm in its place.

'Where's Brian Jackson now?' she asked, suddenly resenting that he let Barney work on his own like this.

'Oh, he went off home. He'll like this better when he sees it tomorrow, if he'll listen, of course.'

'What are you doing now?' Deborah asked him.

'Me? Oh just sitting watching this, I suppose. Having a think about it.' He turned and looked at her, pulling his mouth down in an exaggerated, mournful grimace.

'If you stopped getting drunk you'd lose all this grey flesh,' she said and touched his cheek.

'I know, that's right. That's why I'm here; if I don't work then I just go out on the piss. I thought I'd get something of my own going again. I'd better, anyway, or I'll get the bloody sack.'

'Come on,' she said and stood up. 'I'll make you a cup of tea.' She waited while he turned off lights, locked doors, checked windows.

'Animal bloody rights activists,' he grumbled, 'bloody vegiburger brigade. Half the arty bastards in this university. Shut it down, I would. That Les, Les Holland, wasted he is grubbing about after those Victorian poofters. Thomas sodding Hardy,' he said accusingly. 'Have you read him?' She shook her head, grinning at his bad temper. 'Load of crap.' He rattled the door. 'There we go,' and turned to her, put his arm over her shoulders and walked her down the

141

yellow-lit pathway to the footbridge.

'Mind you,' he went on, 'some of it's okay; Jacobeans, lots of blood and sex, worth saving that is. Do you know what they do, though? They've got rows and rows of smelly bloody spinsters, all sweat and bristles, counting sodding commas and conjunctions.' He turned his head and saw her laughing at him.

'You know all about it, do you?' she asked.

'Absolutely. All you've got to do is read it. They're only stories, you know; nothing difficult.' He stopped and stood facing her. 'Structure. That's what they're on about now. What's it all for?' He looked her in the face, demanding an answer.

'Perhaps they like it,' she said reasonably.

'No, they don't, how can they? Miserable bastards, they are.' He grumbled on in pretended bad temper, she laughing at him as they walked into the college buildings.

She shared a kitchen with half a dozen other students. Bernard Guy sat at the round formica-topped table and watched Deborah.

Les Holland walked from the station. He put his suitcase down on the pavement and fiddled around for his keys. There were only a few cars on Micklegate, it was a warm, still evening. When he shut the door behind him he was suddenly in darkness. He leaned back against the door and stood for a few seconds in the silence. He turned on the light and the dirty staircase sprang up.

In his room his books were there, open on the desk, waiting for him. A couple of hours, he thought, and I can still have half an hour in the pub. He found a bottle of beer in the kitchen, came back and sat down. He picked his way into the print, sat reading, humming to himself, drinking his beer.

He got into the Falcon at just after ten o'clock. The room seemed distant from him. He was strained and a little tired from reading; the light seemed paler than it really was. Leaning on the bar he ordered a pint of bitter and stood on his own drinking it. He put his glass down on the dark, polished wood; someone put another glass down beside it so that their hands nearly touched. Les looked up, starting back almost.

'Evening, Les,' said Robert Devonshire.

'Why, Sergeant, what a delightful surprise,' said Les smoothly.

'Ready for another?'

'Why not? Thanks.' Devonshire ordered their drinks and they stood silently, watching the barman pull the beer into straight pint glasses.

'Cheers,' said Les.

'Listen, Les,' Devonshire began.

'Yes, Sergeant.' Les sprang to a false, derisive attentiveness.

'Now, you and your mate Charlie,' Devonshire ploughed on, ignoring the mockery, 'you're not bad lads, stupid more than bad, but then again, I don't know what you're playing at, so perhaps I can't judge. No, be quiet' – he held his finger up to Les's mouth – 'because you don't know how far in the shit you are.'

Les put his glass down, serious for the first time.

'Did you know,' asked Devonshire, 'that you've been followed for the last, what, perhaps two days?' Les smiled at him and started to speak but Devonshire stopped him again. 'No, shut it. This is serious for you. The man who owns the painting that you most certainly have, one of you, is a very big, bad, bad bastard and he's set on you a slimier, bigger,

143

badder bastard who's going to pull your arms and legs off. Now, that painting has got, do you understand, *got* to reappear very sharpish. They might still pull your arms and legs off, of course, just to show you, but you never know.'

Les turned away from Devonshire and stared over the bar at the rows of bottles.

'There's not a lot I can say.' Les turned sideways to look straight at Robert Devonshire. 'Almost anything, apart from something like "I don't understand" or "we haven't got it" means that you'll think the worst. Anyway, why are you bothering?'

Robert Devonshire shrugged. 'Good-hearted, I suppose. I like to be respectable. I'm not like your lot.'

'Bopping Charlie? That's respectable, is it?'

'Oh, come on.'

'Blood, hospitals; you've still got the marks of it.'

'Eric Ellis, that's the guy's name,' said Devonshire, ignoring Les's cleverness. 'Now, he's poked around town; up there at the university he's been at least with all the people I've seen. He knows about Lena whatsit and Charlie boy the burglar. So you see, that leaves you. Now you, you're a right smartarse and he's suddenly not getting anywhere. So, I'm here to say to you, send this painting to Eric Ellis straight away. But you, you're not going to do that, being a smartarse and all. So Ellis, he's going to get a couple of his mates, this is my guess, and they're going to get some red-hot shovels and slip them under your feet.'

'I don't want anything to do with this,' said Les abruptly. 'I wanted to nick the picture, sell it and spend the money. I'm a simple soul. Why's this bugger so keen on this one painting? He can't be poor—'

'People don't like it, having things pinched. It pisses

people off. It's worse when somebody like Charles Wilson does it; he does it for badness. Other people do it for money and that's reasonably okay, but not when it's simply for the pleasure of shitting on people. And you really picked the wrong bloke with this Barker, he's a purler.'

'It's nothing to do with me now. I can't give anything back when I've not got it.'

'You've got to do a lot better than that, you prat.'

'It's difficult.'

Bernard Guy was leaning with his back to a kitchen cupboard. When Deborah handed him his mug of tea he reached out and touched her hip with his left hand.

'You'll spill it,' she said, took half a pace forward and kissed him on the mouth. She turned away from him, picked up her own cup and walked off down the corridor. Barney followed her into her room. She was sitting on the bed. He sat in the armchair and put his tea down on the desk. With the two of them the room was almost full. Deborah slipped off the bed on to her knees. She shuffled to Barney and knelt upright between his legs.

'Don't tell me though,' said Robert Devonshire. 'If you do, I'll have to do something about it.'

Les looked at him in surprise. 'Bit of a change. What's happened to you?'

Devonshire ignored the question. 'This Ellis,' he said, 'he'll be at the Manor Hotel. Go and see him. Take him the picture, for God's sake.'

'I can't,' said Les miserably.

The shower was hot on Barney's back; he squirted the

145

shower gel on to Deborah's breasts and gently rubbed it into a white foam. He spread his hands over her shoulders and pulled her to him, his hands over her wet, soapy back, sliding on to her buttocks.

Les sat on his own in the kitchen. The bareness and silence drove him into his own room. There was a record on the turntable and he started it without looking. It was George Formby. It cheered him up, listening to it, thinking about Deborah.

CHAPTER TWENTY-FIVE

There wasn't a readable book in the library. Charles sat in the middle of the room and fiddled with the switches on his wheelchair's armrest and spun slowly round. It was a dark, grubby room, little used. The walls carried shelves of books and two or three dusty pictures. He picked up the telephone which lay in his lap, pressed a button, listened and said, 'Eileen, this library: I'm going to get rid of it. Get on the phone, would you, and find a bookseller and a builder.'

He sent the chair over to the window and looked out across a terrace of cracked, dark stone, a rough lawn and trees which straggled up the hillside, thickening into dense woodland as the ground rose. He heard the door open and shut behind him. Eileen said, 'Why do you want a builder? I'll have to give them some idea of what you want.'

Charles spun himself round and looked at her, pale and belligerent, dressed in tee-shirt, cut off jeans and trainers. 'A gymnasium,' he said. 'All those machines, you know, a sauna and so on.' She looked at him, unsmiling, sulking, he thought. 'Good idea?' he asked.

'There's post for you,' she said, 'a parcel, some letters. Do you want them in here?'

'In the kitchen,' he said, deflated. You bloody wait, he

thought, wait till I get out of this bloody chair. I'll make you bloody squeal.

She left doors open behind her and he buzzed through them into the kitchen. It was a kitchen built for a staff, a massive room now lined with modern cupboards and drawers, work tops and machines. In the middle was a heavy wooden table littered with paper, vases, pens, cups, plates.

'There you are,' said Eileen briskly and pushed over to him a large, flat, oblong parcel. On it were three envelopes.

'Well,' said Charles when he'd seen the postmark, 'I know what's in that.' And he began to read his letters.

Celia's letter hurt him the most. It was a get-well letter, written out of duty by a well-brought-up girl: a little light gossip, conventional concern and indifferently brief. He felt his face tighten.

'What's the matter?' said Eileen. He looked up and saw her looking at him across the table. He flicked the letter over to her and watched as she read it.

'Well?'

'Contempt,' he said and when he saw her blank expression went on, 'Celia writes subtext. She's letting me see her give me a passing glance; a polite, sympathetic smile that she's managed, but only barely, to find time for.'

'Don't be stupid, it's only a bit of a letter.'

'That's right.'

'Subtext,' he heard her mutter as she turned to crack an egg into the frying pan. 'Who's Celia then, what's she do, apart from this subtext crap, that is?'

'Never mind,' said Charles. 'You're right.' He sat back and watched her cooking, watched her shoulder moving under the cotton tee-shirt.

'What's in the parcel?'

'It's the precious painting that Les and I stole when we were art thieves.'

'Is it then?'

Charles opened the brown paper parcel, picked his way through the sheets of cardboard and Sellotape and there was the painting.

'Here you are,' he said, 'come and have a look at it. It's not bad, you know. I thought I didn't like this chap, but it's pretty good.' Eileen looked down at the painting, fish slice in one hand.

'Looks sour,' she said.

'Don't drip fat on it, Eileen.'

'What are you going to do with it?'

'Well.' Charles grinned and rubbed his hands together. 'I thought I could sneak back to York and plant it in Frank Vernon's house or his study and then denounce him to the police.' He looked up at her, eyes wide, waiting for judgement. 'But, you know, I might just keep it.'

'Good idea, that,' said Eileen dryly. 'What does your mate Les say?'

'Oh, well.'

'Oh, well, what?'

'He did say, before I went through the roof, that he wasn't keen.'

'End of a beautiful friendship,' she said flatly.

'Not for me,' said Charles softly. He looked up into Eileen's face. 'Les is pure.'

'Pure?' said Eileen, tapping the fish slice on the table in annoyance.

'So, he'll go off on his own and brood, or something like that.'

'How can he be pure?'

'He'll be trotting out the romantic concepts for himself: honour, betrayal and so on.'

'Sounded a dirty little sod to me.'

'To you he probably would be,' said Charles, smiling.

'What?'

'A dirty little sod. He'd want your knickers off, no doubt about it.'

Eileen stood with her hands on her hips, fish slice sticking out of her fist. 'And what about you then?'

'No,' Charles said. 'He's not much interested in my knickers.' She turned away.

'Beef burgers?' she asked. 'Or just a fried egg sandwich?'

'I think he's probably right,' said Eric Ellis. He crossed his legs and leaned back in his chair. Across the desk from him sat Wayne Barker. His usual high colour was flushed, there was sweat on his face. He wiped it with the end of the pale blue towel which was draped around his neck.

'I'm going to have a shower, Eric.' He stood up. His square torso stretched out his tee-shirt in tight creases, showing flesh and black, curly hair above his tracksuit trousers. 'Ten minutes,' he said and left Ellis alone in the office.

'Sod it,' said Ellis. He followed Barker through the open door into the small flat which adjoined his office. It was like a room in a motorway hotel but grubby and untidy. The pictures on the walls were real pictures and there was a poster advertising an exhibition of Raoul Dufy's paintings pinned over the bedside table. Barker was sitting on the bed, taking off his running shoes. He scooped off his socks.

'What's up, Eric?'

'I'm fed up of this,' said Ellis. 'I've told you, I've spoken to this sergeant, what's his name, Devonshire? It's more or less

150

certain that this other kid, the one that fell through the roof, that he's the one with the picture. The Holland character, he's out of it, or at least he's not the best bet.'

Wayne Barker stood up and took off his tracksuit trousers. 'Go on then, Eric, what do you want to do?' He pulled the tee-shirt over his head and stood looking aggressively at Ellis.

'Well, how about going and taking it off him?'

'What a good idea.' Barker sat on the bed and pulled his jock strap off. 'What if he won't give it to you?' He was mumbling as he tugged at the elastic waist band.

'We'll beat the shit out of him until he does,' said Ellis impatiently. 'It's not that complicated.' Barker looked up at him from where he was sitting on the bed, pointed a finger at him.

'No,' he said, sharply. And then, patiently, 'It is complicated.' He stood up and walked across the room to Ellis. He put his hands on Ellis's shoulders. 'And you're not to get cross with this boy.'

'There's no real problem, fortunately,' said Charles Wilson. 'We're on the ground floor and the house is so solid anyway.'

'Who bought all these books?' asked Les Holland. 'It's all crap.'

'They accumulated: grandfathers and uncles and so on.'

'Collected sermons,' said Les, looking at a shelf of brown leather bindings. 'Are they worth anything?'

'Oh, yes.'

'Amazing.' Les sat down in an armchair. Charles stood near him, balancing on metal crutches. 'I'm surprised you're up.'

'Up?'

'Not in bed. You know, still injured.' Les was awkward.

'I am still injured.'

'Not very much. At one time I was getting ready to put a pillow over your face.'

'Will you be able to get rid of the flat?'

'No problem. We packed all your stuff. Pickfords. They should be delivering it here.'

'Can we stop this?' Charles turned round, away from Les and swung himself towards the door. 'Come on, shit head, let's have a drink. It's not a big deal, nothing's happened.' He went through the door. 'Come on, Les, for Christ's sake.' Les got up and followed him across the hall, into the long dining room and then into the kitchen.

'Where's the nurse?'

'Eileen? She's sunbathing. There's a sun trap on the other side of the house. It's good for me; I do a lot of it now.'

'You screwing her?'

'That's my boy.'

Charles used the crutches to the front door and sat in the wheelchair which was outside on the flagged terrace.

'Take the sticks, Les. I walk a bit each day but the wheels are a lot easier.'

'You've got to make an effort, Chas,' said Les earnestly.

'Shut up.' Charles pressed the buttons and rolled silently off. Les followed him.

'It's all right this,' Les shouted. He stopped and looked round, at the wild-looking woods on the hillside in the distance, the hot blue sky. He walked along by the side of the house, following Charles. When he turned the corner the terrace continued downwards in broad steps into a sunken garden topped on two sides by a right-angled wall of old, dressed stone. Charles was waiting, in the chair, at the top of the steps.

'I can get down with the sticks but it's easier with a piggy back.'

When they got to the bottom of the steps Les suddenly saw Eileen. He stood over her as she lay on a blanket on the grass.

'You're not very brown,' he said.

'She puts on a lot of cream,' said Charles.

'That should make her brown.'

'Not necessarily, it's a barrier cream. She's a Celt, you see, pale skin.'

'Her nipples are brown.'

'Not another word,' said Eileen without opening her eyes.

'Everybody's nipples are brown,' said Charles.

'Mine are pink.'

'Don't like the sound of that. Come on, put me down. Gently, you sod.' Charles hopped, held on to Les's arm and sat down next to Eileen. He pulled his tee-shirt off over his head and lay back on the grass.

'You look all right,' said Les.

'The scars are fading; I've got good skin. That's what the doctor says.'

'You're all right?'

'Wonderful.'

'What about the trial?'

'Hardly a trial.'

'What happened?' said Les impatiently. Charles made a face and sighed.

'Probation.'

'You what?'

'It was good old Frank Vernon. The witless sod sent such a report of my behaviour that no one could have thought me even halfway sane. The probation officer went as far as saying, in court, that it was Frank's fault for not helping me, getting me some treatment earlier. I've had a breakdown and the university's to blame. Complete rest under medical supervision.'

'That's me,' said Eileen softly.

'A year off and then I can finish my degree.'

'You bastard,' said Les, disgusted.

'You'd have got six months. Being a bit upper crust, I've got a psychiatrist and the GP and the naughty nurse to look after me.'

They sat on the lawn drinking beer. Les fell asleep, was startled awake when Charlie slapped cold suntan cream on his chest.

'Don't get burned,' Charlie told him. Les rubbed the cream over his chest and shoulders.

'Where's Eileen?'

'Cooking.'

'Such a help when you can get good staff.'

Just above a whisper at first, Les started to sing 'Sylvia's Mother'. Then, fists clenched, straining at the words like Dr Hook.

'For God's sake.' Charlie looked across at him.

'Best pop song ever written,' Les told him.

'Who says that?'

'My dad.'

'That's it, then. That Mrs Adrian was a cow, though.' Charles lay back on the grass. The sky was heavy, ready to fall. 'This summer, what shall we do?'

'I'm going to work for my dad. Two weeks, maybe three. They're going to America.'

'They're going where?'

'This summer, Florida. They let scruffs in now, you know.'
Then he sang again, louder, shouting. Charles howled and
sobbed with him.

'You know it, then?'

'Course I do. It's the best pop song ever written.' Les
looked. 'Your dad told me. He always tells me. Every time he
puts it on the juke box in the pub he and the barman, what's
his name, Billy, they both tell me.'

CHAPTER TWENTY-SIX

'We ought to have kept it,' said Les. 'It's a wonderful flat.' He sat on one of the tin trunks and looked across the kitchen at Deborah.

'No,' she said.

'What do you mean, "no"?'

'It's a crappy flat: two rooms, a kitchen and a bathroom, traffic noise, fumes. It's dusty and shitty.'

'Leaves and bits of grass and all that; bloody birds, that's what you rate, isn't it?'

'There's no need to be nasty. That's what you do, you turn on people.'

Les Holland walked across the room and grabbed her by the lapel of her jacket. 'Where am I going to live next year?'

She turned squarely to him so that their faces were close. 'When?'

'Next year.'

'Oh, come on, it's nearly four months away.'

Les let go of her and stepped back. He looked away for an instant and then, abrupt and awkward, 'Let's get a flat together.'

'No way.'

'Oh, well, Christ, why don't you just say what you mean?'

157

'I'm not playing house with you.' She walked around him in a half circle, hands raised in an angry gesture. 'No, don't start this. Just don't pout.'

'I'm fucking well hurt, I am.'

'Good, serves you right.'

Les sat on the kitchen table, tucked his hands under his thighs. 'We nicked all this you know,' he told Deborah. 'Well, not all.' She crossed from the window and sat with him, holding his arm. He laughed. 'We hired a van, do-it-yourself removals. They give you these big cardboard boxes.'

Charlie had laughed when Les told him the plan.

'Great stuff,' he had said. 'Come on then.' Les had stopped him.

'Tea time we'll do it; Friday afternoon, late. It'll be dead quiet.'

Charlie had laughed. 'You've worked it out, then?'

'Course I have.'

They had parked the van outside the porters' lodge of Goodricke College. 'They don't know us here, do they?' Les had explained. 'And keep your mouth shut, they don't have lah-de-dah removal men.'

'We just strolled in,' he told Deborah. 'Charlie was laughing, I mean, really howling the bugger was. We stripped one of the guest rooms. Even got the double mattress. Wrapped it up in polythene and whizzed it out. Went through one of the kitchens, you know, toaster, kettle and so on. If I'd thought about a screwdriver we could have had tables, wardrobes.' Les laughed, turning to her. 'Bloody porter holding the door open for us, Charlie pissing himself. I wanted to shoot off fast. Charlie kept going back in: light shades, shower fittings, one of those little cooker things.' He stopped. Deborah kissed him. She kissed his cheek, as though he were a child. He shook his head. 'It was brilliant,' he said softly. 'We had glasses on and flat caps.' He wiped his eyes on his shirt sleeve. 'Hope he's okay.'

Les went and sat on the window sill. 'Where am I going to live? It took months to get this place.'

'There are hundreds of rooms up at that university. They're built for students. You're a student. Go up there next year, be a monk, get a first. Isn't that it?' He tried to speak, but she shouted at him, stamping in anger. 'On your own, not with that shitbag.'

Les said nothing. He looked down at the floor. He wouldn't have a friend like Charlie again, he knew that.

'Charlie's no good when he's not on the go,' he said. 'Diving around, inventing dramas. You know what I mean?'

'No.'

'When we went nicking things, there was never a problem, smooth, confident.'

'He's a cruel sod.'

'Not to me.'

'Oh, well, that's fine, then. He picks on people.'

'Course he does.'

'They're all weaker than he is.'

'Most people are; that's what puts him in a bad light. It's only coincidence though; he'd pick on King Kong if he came down the street. But King Kongs are a bit thin on the ground.'

'He's simply practising on the rest of us, is he?'

'I suppose he is.'

'You're bloody mad. You're serious, aren't you?'

'Course I am. Look, he even has a go at fighting people and, Christ, he's crap at it.' He smiled at her, shrugged, and turned to the window. 'We'll load the rest of his stuff in the car, shall we?' Deborah stood with her hands in her jacket pockets.

'Well, at least you like the car.' She stared at him. 'You do, you said you did.'

'It's ridiculous,' she said.

'It's a very nice motor. Fiats are good cars. We can go to Italy in it.'

'They do let you in without one.'

'I'll sell it when we get back.'

Deborah looked at him coldly. 'Pick the bags up,' she said.

They were sitting round a table in the corner of the bar. The juke box made everyone shout. Packed and sweaty, the end of term.

'I'm off tomorrow,' said Celia, drunk. 'From Heathrow.'

'We could meet you in Paris,' said Deborah. 'I'm afraid Les will be with me.'

'Good,' said Celia. 'I like Les.' She leaned across the table and pulled Les away from the two girls he was talking to and kissed him on the mouth.

'Something I said?' he asked, bewildered.

'Come to Paris with me, Les. Leave Deborah and come off with me.'

'Okay.'

'We can stay in my mother's flat.'

'Sounds wonderful. Another drink?'

'Completely unnecessary. Screw all afternoon.'

'It's a shame, but I'm afraid I really have arranged to have Deborah with me now.' He smiled nastily at Deborah.

'Screw her in the evening,' She sat back and grinned glassily at Deborah. 'Give us a kiss,' she said.

Les went to the bar and shoved his way forward into the light. 'Now then, Barney.' Bernard Guy turned round from the bar and stared stonily at him. 'No, Barney, don't say anything cruel. I am a good person. I no longer take the piss out of fat, middle-aged losers. I no longer involve them in art theft, nor steal from them, nor do I say cutting things. I buy them large gin and tonics and put my arms round them.' Les Holland put his arm across Barney's shoulders and shouted at the barmaid. Barney smiled.

Eric Ellis sat in the back of the black Ford Granada. 'The turn's on your right, George,' he said. 'About half a mile now.'

The hedges flicked past on either side of a sunken lane. Outside the glow from the dashboard and the car's headlights, it was dark. Ellis leaned forward. 'Steady on; there we are.'

The car bumped over a ridge of grass and stones and into the narrow driveway. It was only wide enough for one vehicle. There were two passing places cut out from the thick mass of rhododendrons. 'When you get to the bend you can see the house, so turn your lights off.' George stopped the car and they sat in darkness.

'Better to walk down, Eric.'

Eric Ellis sat back. He turned to the man at his side. 'Peter,' he said, 'no nonsense, no mess.'

'You keep saying. George has told me.'

'Lots of menace, fear. And do remember he's a lippy little sod; he's going to say lots of clever things. You're not to damage him, we want what we want without fuss. That means no self-indulgence.'

'All right, all right, message received,' said Peter gruffly. 'Mind you, can't see why not, start chopping fingers and toes off and you don't half speed things up. Joke,' he added hastily as he saw Ellis's face.

161

They got out of the car and stood in the cool, dark night, Ellis small and nimble between the bulk of the other two. As they walked down the drive towards the dark shape of the house they stumbled into each other before their eyes became accustomed to the night and they found their balance on the rutted surface.

Closer, they could see that there were lights behind the heavily curtained windows. They stood under the wooden porch and Ellis rang the bell.

Charles Wilson didn't freeze when they banged past the opening door and into the house. He rolled around the door-way that led into the library and slammed the heavy door. They heard the lock clatter and stood in the hall looking at four closed doors and the staircase. Ellis pointed at the two doors to their left. The two big men took a door each, opened it, stepped into the rooms. Peter came out, shook his head at Ellis.

'No,' said George briefly.

The third door led them into a wide corridor; on the left hand wall were glass-fronted cabinets of books. There were doors to their right. The corridor finished at a heavy wooden door with a letter box in it. The first door was locked. The second led them into a long dining room filled with a single polished table and upholstered dining chairs. Beyond them was another door.

'Corridor, George,' said Ellis. 'Watch both outside doors.' George stepped back into the corridor. 'He's got to be in the kitchen.' Ellis pointed at the far door.

There were two doors, a tiny room insulating the kitchen from the dining room. The doors had no locks.

'He'll be on the phone,' said Peter shrilly.

'Bet you he won't.'

162

Charles was in the kitchen. He was sitting so that the table was between them. As Peter came through the door Charles closed the shotgun and pointed it at him.

Les stayed at the bar with Barney.

'Forget it, Les,' said Barney.

'But it's right, Barney, you were good with the painting. You did it, not bottling out. And we just stood about taking the piss.'

'Okay, now be quiet, you did me a good turn.'

'No, it was all a failure.' Les leaned on the bar, sipped his beer. 'Sorry about the grand, Barney.'

'I've always responded well to contempt.'

'You what?'

'Gets me going, sorts me out. I can't bear it.'

'What does?'

'Never mind, Les.' Barney looked at him, said softly, 'You'll see.' He stood back from the bar. 'See you next year, Les. Have a nice summer.'

'Celia's having a little zizz,' said Deborah when Les sat down again.

'Want this?' said Les, handing her a glass.

'What is it?'

'Barney's gin, never touched it.' He looked at Celia. Her head was back and she was leaning to one side, her throat white and open. He reached out and touched it with the tips of his fingers. 'Celia's lovely,' he said.

'She'll be lovely and heavy when we have to carry her upstairs.'

'Did you see Barney?' asked Les.

'What about him?' Deborah sipped the gin. 'It's neat gin, this.' She shuffled along the seat and stood up, pushed tight against Les by the press of people in the bar. Les reached up and slid his hand over her back and, as she walked away, she left his hand trailing after her in the air.

He looked across at Celia. Her eyes opened, caught his glance.

'That was a nice thing to hear,' she said and she shut her eyes again. He laid his hand gently on her white throat.

'I'm a nice person,' he said.

Peter was forty-five years old. He was a very strong man and the gun that Charlie pointed at him made him very frightened.

Even though the table which separated him from Charlie was solid and heavy he threw up the edge of it so that the incline of its top was in Charlie's face and knocked up the shotgun. Peter tried to tip the table over on to Charlie but the weight of it was too much. The legs screeched over the floor driving Charlie backwards and then overturning him. Charlie pulled both triggers at once. In a flurry of panic Peter threw his edge of the table up into the noise. The opposite edge of the table cracked into Charlie's chest as he lay face upwards on the stone-flagged floor of the kitchen.

Eric Ellis was following Peter into the kitchen. He could see the bottom of the table and Charlie's body pinned beneath it. 'Pull it off him,' he shouted. He put his foot against the end of one of the legs. 'Pull that edge back.'

Peter looked at him blankly. 'The fucker had a gun.'

'Pull it.'

The table banged down square on its legs again. They could see Charlie's face now; he was staring popeyed. His mouth and chin were covered in blood. It was soaking into his tee-shirt. They could see the dull colour of it advancing as more of the shirt became sodden.

164

★ ★ ★

'Hold her up, dammit,' hissed Deborah. Les leaned over Celia, put his arms round her waist and tried to lift her hips up off the bed.

'Pull them off,' he said, his voice muffled as his face was half flattened on to Celia's stomach. He slid a hand down under her jeans, trying to ease them over her buttocks. Deborah pulled again and got the jeans off.

'Right, hold her up,' she said to Les. 'Go on, get behind her and prop her up so that I can get her blouse off.'

'What for? She's all right.'

'She'll feel terrible if she sleeps in her clothes.'

Les tried to pull her up by her arms.

'Get behind her and shove her upright,' Deborah ordered him.

Celia wrapped her arms round Les's neck. She licked his ear. 'You undress me, Les,' she mumbled.

'You're right,' said Deborah. 'She's all right as she is.' Les looked at her, grinning. 'Out,' said Deborah, but she was laughing.

'Another time,' he said to Celia.

He waited in the corridor until Deborah came out of her room. She had a large canvas bag over her shoulder, a red sleeping bag under her arm.

'Well,' he said, 'that's your bed taken. Where do we go?'

'We'll get some cushions from the armchairs in the common room, we can sleep outside by the lake.'

'Give over.'

'It's a warm night. You're too pissed to drive your silly car.' She kissed him and took his hand.

CHAPTER TWENTY-SEVEN

Les sat behind the counter in his father's shop. The counter was formed by the glass top of a showcase of watches. There were cabinets of rings, brooches, watches on each of the walls. The shop was so tiny that it was almost a cubicle. Les looked up at the middle-aged woman in front of him.

'How long?' she said, incredulously.

'A week,' said Les. 'Well, round about that.'

'I can't wait, really. It's now I want it.' Her silver-blonde hair was rigid when she moved her head.

'I can do it.'

'Not sure about that, love. Skilled man, your dad. I've been coming here years, you know. No, I'd better wait. Where is he?'

'Wyoming.'

'Oh yes,' she said sceptically. Les stared at her. She looked at him uncertainly for some seconds.

'Bye, then,' said Les flatly and stared her out of the door. I'm fed up of this, he thought.

He went back to his book but the door opened again. He looked up and saw first the light brown skirt, the white blouse and then the pale, tight face. 'Morning,' he said. The girl said nothing, she stared at him, disbelieving, pressing against the counter, leaning over him.

'It's me,' she said quietly.

'Course it is.'

'Don't be smart, Les.'

'Eileen?' He looked properly at her. 'Christ, what's up?'

'They've killed Charlie.'

'You what? Don't come . . .' Then he stopped, looked down at the book on his lap. He could see the shape of the verse on the page; the words were indistinguishable.

The door opened and shut and a tall, thin man came into the shop. He looked in the display case to his left.

'I'd like to see this brooch, please,' he said to Les. Les came from behind the counter, unlocked the case and took out the brooch. It was a dark blue ceramic in an oval, silver frame. He put it in a box, took the man's money, thanked him, walked him to the door and locked it behind him.

'Who killed him?'

'Friday night,' said Eileen. 'I was upstairs, in the bath. He fired the shotgun and there was a lot of noise, banging about, downstairs. I waited till it was quiet, then I went down.'

'No,' Les whispered. 'Say it quickly.'

'He was dead, in the kitchen. I looked at him. His chest was crushed and the back of his head. I phoned the cops and then I sat with him till they came.' He could see her there in the bleak kitchen, waiting with Charlie.

'Were you frightened?' he said stupidly.

'Of course I was.' She was crying, making a soft, breathless noise in her throat as she tried to make herself calm.

'What did they say, the cops?'

'They didn't say much, not to me. People trying to burgle the place.' She shrugged hopelessly. 'I bet it wasn't, was it?'

Les stood in the shop with his arms folded tightly across his chest, crying forlornly.

Then he couldn't cry and stood with his eyes closed, finding himself again.

'I don't know when the funeral is,' said Eileen, 'with the police and all that.'

'I wouldn't go anyway,' said Les.

'It's this picture of yours, isn't it, that's what they were after Charlie for?'

Les nodded at her. 'Course it was,' he said. 'But killing him for it.'

'They didn't get it,' said Eileen. 'It's in my bag at the station.'

Les didn't think at all. He said, 'Let's go and get it then. Then you get on a train and vanish.'

'Just like that?' She burst into tears again.

'You don't need this any more than I do. So go back to London, get a job and forget it. I know it's rotten,' he said quietly.

He locked the shop and they stood on the pavement outside until a taxi stopped for them.

It was late afternoon when Les Holland got into York. He drove in through Micklegate past the flat where he and Charlie had lived, down through the city and parked outside Barney's house. He rang the bell and stood waiting on the doorstep. The door opened and Barney stood in the doorway, square and uninviting.

'Can I come in, Barney?'

'No, Les, you can't.'

'You what?'

'I'm finished with all that.'

Les hung his head. 'Look, Barney, it's important.'

'Oh shit.'

'Come on, let me in.'

'No, Les, no. Go on, push off.' Barney put his hands to his head. 'No more of it.'

'Fuck you then,' said Les and walked away.

He drove out of the city and north up the A1 until he found a motel. He told the girl who was at the reception desk that he would be leaving early, paid her and asked for a call at five-thirty.

He lay on the bed and watched television. When the news came on at nine o'clock he went down to the restaurant and ate hamburger steak and cauliflower, drank a bottle of red wine. He went back to his room and lay in bed thinking about Charlie until he went to sleep.

It was still gloomy when he arrived at the university. He parked the car on a piece of rough ground under a spread of tall trees. They dripped glumly on to the car roof as Les sat waiting for the sky to lighten, the cleaners to arrive. If anyone saw him he could say he was from an overnight delivery firm; he had even put a packet of brown envelopes in his pocket to wave at them. He couldn't bring himself to care much about it.

The air was cold and he reached back into the car for his jacket. He got out and walked to the road from where he could see the white walls of the college buildings behind a screen of shrubs and slender trees. The lights were on. It was easy to walk across the narrow lawn, through the bits of shrubbery and on to the paved pathway edging the building which housed the philosophy department.

Les knew that they never locked the seminar room. That would have to do unless he was lucky.

He went up the bare, open stairway. There was the buzz of a vacuum cleaner from the far end of the corridor when he went through the double doors. The corridor was empty, the doors of the offices on either side of it were open. Les went back through the doors and waited on the landing. When the cleaner came from an office into the corridor the boom of the machine became louder, was muffled as she went into the next office. When the noise dimmed for the third time Les looked through the doors again, saw the corridor empty and walked quickly up it, saw the back of the cleaner in her nylon overall in the office next to Frank Vernon's. He went into Vernon's office and squatted on the floor behind his dark oak desk. He tried the roll top and found that it was locked.

He was carrying the painting as he had before. The tape came painfully off his chest. With one hand he held the painting against the underside of the kneehole of the desk and with the other smoothed the tape on to the rough surface of the wood. From the reel in his pocket he tore off two fresh lengths of tape and stuck them diagonally across the polythene-covered painting, fixing it firmly.

Les stood up, fastened his shirt and coat. The vacuum cleaner stopped. He didn't notice at first, but as he came to the door he realised. He stood, stupidly, heart pounding; a door closed and then keys jangled as the whole bunch turned with the key in the lock. Then another door. Les went and knelt again behind the desk. The light went out; he heard the door being locked.

The window slid open easily and he could see the road through the thin foliage. He eased himself out of the window, straight-armed, his toes scraping the brickwork; then the weight on to his forearms, hanging by hands, fingers, letting go. His feet hit the ground and he fell backwards into the hawthorn. He could stand, he was all right, scratched, breathless.

He drove straight back to Northampton, had a bath, had breakfast, walked down Wellingborough Road into town and opened up his father's shop for the day.

Bernard Guy lay in bed reading the *Guardian* and drinking tea. The blue velvet curtains were parted slightly and he could see that the morning was dull and wet. He could hear Deborah in the bathroom slamming the cupboard door that he knew would never shut. He was reading about cricket when she came into the room.

'I can't find your talcum powder,' she said. 'I don't want to unpack mine again.'

'It's on top of the cabinet; might be a bit high for you.' He looked up and saw her going back through the door, saw that she was naked. 'Deborah,' he shouted.

'Too late, buster,' she shouted back. 'You should look at people when you're talking to them.' He was out of bed and running, knowing that she'd lock the bathroom door. He caught her, picked her up, staggered with her into the bedroom and fell backwards on to the bed. She landed on top of him, his face pressing into her flesh.

At lunch time Les went into the Central Library in Northampton and found Robert Devonshire's number in the York telephone directory. He might be on nights or something, thought Les. He telephoned from the shop but there was only Devonshire's wife. He asked when would be a good time to phone back. She thought early evening but it was hard to be sure. Who was phoning? Les told her it was Wyndham Lewis and rang off.

Big Soft Lads

★ ★ ★

'It's none of your business, Barney,' said Deborah tartly.

'Oh, come on, you must admit it's odd.'

'It's not odd, Barney. Not odd at all. Pretty well normal, I wouldn't mind betting.'

Barney drove on in silence. Below them a sweep of empty moorland sloped off bleakly into the rain. He didn't like the thought of Les standing there on his doorstep pleading with him while Deborah was sitting inside watching television.

'Don't be morose, Barney, you're my bit on the side,' said Deborah cheerfully. 'Bits on the side should be happy or they're no damn good to anybody.'

It's only for the weekend, thought Barney.

Les sat in his red Fiat outside Robert Devonshire's house. He had sat for almost an hour and was listening to *The Archers* when Devonshire walked past the car. Les sounded the horn. It shrieked in the quiet, leafy street. Devonshire peered in through the side window. Les rolled it down and before Devonshire could speak said, 'Get in. I've lots to tell you.'

Devonshire looked up and down the street. 'Better be good.'

'Do as you're fucking told,' Les hissed at him. Devonshire stared, puzzled, straightened up from the window, walked round the front of the car and got in.

'Drive,' he said to Les. 'Get us away from my house, you stupid sod.'

Les waited until they were on the ring road and he could cruise along before he told Devonshire what he wanted him to do.

'Sergeant,' he said, 'these bastards you've been working for, you know the ones you told me about in the pub . . .'

'I'm not working for anybody.' Devonshire stuck his finger in Les's face. 'Don't you go bloody saying that.'

'They've been down to Charlie's place and they've murdered him. Like you threatened.'

Devonshire sat back in his seat. 'You little shit,' he said. Then he took in the words. 'They've done what? They've killed him?'

'They don't come deader than Charlie.' They came to a roundabout, Les went all the way round and headed back towards York. 'All I want you to do, well it's silly really, Sergeant Devonshire. I'll give you the painting and I'll not tell anyone about your goings on with Wayne Barker and all. But you've got to persecute somebody for me. I don't suppose you'll get as far as prosecution, that would be too much to hope for, but you've got to be as shitty as possible.'

'Is that all?'

'That's it.'

'What for?'

'For Charlie's bit of fun,' said Les softly.

He told Devonshire what he knew about Charlie's death as they drove. When they got to the end of the street where Devonshire lived he stopped the car. Devonshire unlocked the door and before he got out he held out his hand to Les. Les shook it.

'I'm sorry about Charlie,' said Devonshire.

CHAPTER TWENTY-EIGHT

I don't know what to do, Les thought. He sat at the corner of the bar and sipped his beer while the clatter of Saturday night went on around him.

'Been working, have you?' Billy asked him as he waited for a pint of Guinness to pour. 'Be a change for you,' he said, pleasantly.

'It's a good shop. Dad's right, people have been fighting to give me money today. Queuing up with fistfuls of notes, it's knackering.'

'Silly buggers,' said Billy, closing the tap with a flick. 'It's all money these days.'

'It'll end in tears,' said Les, but Billy had gone. Les saw him pick notes from the fat fingers of an upturned fist. There were three or four more hands at the bar with crumpled notes, empty glasses.

I'll take Mick for his walk, thought Les, and come back here for the last half hour.

He sat on a bench in the park. Mick ran up to him, sniffed, checking he was there and turned swiftly, running over the path, across the grass, into the dark. Les sat there, thinking about Charlie. He could feel Charlie, his cold, sneering honesty. Only me, he thought, only me. He could feel the beer in him, knew it was making him soft, but he sat still, thinking about Charlie. Charlie and Celia. Does Celia know? he thought. He could ring her in Paris. She was pissed with Charlie. She still loved him though, thought Les. Where was Deborah? Her mother said she was still in York. She wasn't, he knew. She had said she was going home.

'Who should I say called?' her mother had said.

Deborah lay across the narrow bed. She put her right leg over Barney's back, kicking him with her heel, driving him into her.

Les was sitting on a bench in the park watching the darkness in the trees. I don't know what to do, he thought. And he thought of Charlie lying somewhere in the dark, bound and fixed. He fell forward on to his knees, holding his head. Mick's nose, wet, the tongue rough and warm on his face. Les held the dog's head and rubbed its loose, smooth ears. 'Come on then, love,' he said and got up from the bench.

He walked Mick up the grassy slope towards the house. They waited at the kerbside and crossed the road. He took the dog round by the back door and sat with him in the kitchen. Mick drank from his bowl, slapping his tongue into the water then lay down on his blanket under the table.

Les sat and watched the dog, watched it pant, its head sink, watched it fall asleep.

No one will tell Celia, he thought. He found the telephone directory in the pantry and phoned International Directory Enquiries and then sat looking at the number, wondering what he would say. When he rang there was no answer.

It was getting cold outside, he felt it as soon as he stepped out. When he got to the pub he was shivering and then he realised that he was crying.

Deborah put on a sweater over her shirt.

'You'll need that,' said Barney. 'We're high up here.'

She laughed and said, 'It's not far to the pub, though, is it?' She put her arm through his and pulled him to the door. 'Come on you, poor old thing, all worn out, are we?'

Barney reached across her and turned her, by the shoulder, towards him. Deborah stepped in close and kissed him.

If I hadn't sent him the picture, Les thought, then they wouldn't have killed him. If I'd given it back.

'Drink up, Les,' said Billy. Les sat on at the bar as the people drained away. He said goodnight to Billy and went outside into the street, the drink weighing down on him. The doors closed behind him and he heard the bolts rattle. Les walked home under the yellow lights, wandering a little on the pavement, feeling the blame for it all settling sourly into his stomach. When he got in Mick looked up at him, then closed his eyes again. Les thought about the phone but went upstairs and slept.

Deborah lay naked on the settee in front of the fire. She sipped the cognac that Barney had given her and placed the foot of the glass on her stomach. The glass was cold on her skin. She put her legs over the arm so that she could lie flat. Without her hearing him Barney came back into the room and stood behind the settee, looking down at her. The light of the fire deepened the colour of her skin.

Deborah looked up and saw him. 'What should we do now?' she said.

CHAPTER TWENTY-NINE

'I should think that he's mad because they're going to make cuts in the philosophy department. It would pad out his redundancy money as well.' Les listened to the voice on the phone, demanding, wheedling for a name. 'That I can't say,' said Les, 'but it's definitely a philosopher.' He paused to listen again. 'Monday or Tuesday I'd say; that's when the cops should do it. Oh yes,' he added, 'this bloke, the lecturer, he's a poofter; buggers the students.' He rang off. He picked up his pen and crossed off the *Sun*, checked the number and rang the *Star*; after that he'd try the *Daily Mirror*.

When he had finished on the telephone he took Mick out round the park. He stayed out for over an hour, throwing the ball for the dog, running around himself, putting off making his call to Celia. What could he say to her? Perhaps he should go and see her. It wasn't that far.

He went into the house at last and sat in the kitchen looking at the phone. He picked it off the wall, put it on the kitchen table and punched the number. For an instant he thought that it sounded engaged, then realised that it was ringing out in France. A woman's voice, loud and harsh, said something in French. He asked for Celia, heard the phone banged down and then silence.

'Celia Fergussen,' said Celia.

He asked how she was and shut her up when she shouted at him in surprise. He told her that Charlie was dead. He said it just like that; the words jumped out and said themselves leaving him breathless and confused so that he did not hear what she said to him. Then she asked for his number, said she'd call back and rang off.

He fed the dog, made some bacon sandwiches, ate them, drank some fruit juice. The Sunday papers were on the mat so he sat at the table reading them. It was well over an hour before Celia rang back.

The last thing she said was, 'I shall go to the funeral.' Her voice was solid and composed. She would telephone him again, she said, about the arrangements.

'What arrangements?' said Les into the silence of the kitchen.

Les wandered the house. Mick trailed dismally after him, tail and head drooping. The dog gave it up and lay back under the table, eyes liquid and gloomy.

There was no more Charlie; just like that. There was no more shock in the idea, but the wrongness, the awkwardness, left Les unable to fix his mind on anything. He stood in the garden, staring at the flower beds, pulled some weeds. The sun was shining and Les sat on the lawn. Vaguely he thought about their flat, Charlie and himself mounting raids from it. Charlie, now, bound tight, he kept on thinking, bound up tight, his shoulders squashed in the coffin, cramped, nailed in.

The telephone began ringing in the kitchen. Celia said to him that he must go to Charlie's funeral. To see him finished, she said and wept into the phone. To see him finished. Les waited for her and when she could speak she told him to meet her at Heathrow tomorrow. Find out, find out, she insisted, find out about the funeral and find this nurse again.

'Because I want to know,' she said. 'Because I bloody well want to know.'

Les spent the afternoon on the phone. He finally found Charlie's mother and she told him, curtly, reluctantly, about the funeral. She told him to wear a suit, to wear a tie. He put the phone down and called her a shitbag.

Les saw Celia coming along in the stream of passengers. He could not get to the barrier for the press of people waving and calling out. When, finally, she saw him, he stood looking at her, head on one side, arms dangling. She walked up to him and kissed his cheek.

'Good old Les,' she said. 'Thanks for ringing.' He looked back at her, swallowing the thin taste of nausea in his mouth. Tears ran down his cheeks.

'I'm sorry,' he said. 'I keep doing this. Reminds me of Charlie in the hospital. He kept having a weep you know, shock he said it was. I was okay yesterday, damn it.' He picked up her bag, but she stopped him.

'No, tell me here,' she said. 'Not in the car, not while you're driving, doing other things.'

Les looked around, pointed up at the cafeteria, its jumble of tables, people, luggage. 'Up there,' he said. Celia put her arm through his as they walked. They found a free table that was full of dirty crockery. Celia stacked it on to a tray and put it on the table next to them.

'Come on then, Les,' she said, quietly. Her eyes were blue; he looked into her face and told her how he had been sitting in the shop when Eileen came.

'What did you do with it?' she asked him when he told her

about the painting. When he explained she said, puzzled, 'A prank, you played a prank?'

'I know what it was.'

'What were you thinking of?'

'I was thinking of Charlie. I was thinking of how Frank Vernon would probably react to Charlie's death. I thought of Frank Vernon's thin, flaky flesh and I thought of how lovely Charlie was. It was what I did straight off; you know, reaction.'

Celia sat still, quiet. She reached over the table and took Les's hand, kissed it and held it to her cheek.

'It's not enough,' she said and he could feel her tears on his knuckles.

'It won't be for some time,' said Les as they drove up the motorway to Northampton. 'There's an inquest and so on, so the funeral will be God knows when.'

'Can you shut the shop, are you stuck with it?'

'They'll be back on Friday.'

'Will they mind if I'm there?'

'Don't be silly,' said Les. 'My mother thinks you're wonderful.' Les smiled at her and she kissed his cheek again.

'Celia,' he said. 'Celia, I know who killed Charlie.' She froze against him. He could feel her breath on his face. 'It's not enough. I know that. Playing a prank on Frank Vernon. It's not enough.'

CHAPTER THIRTY

'My father shoots,' said Celia. Les tried not to tremble as he poured her coffee. 'He's boorish and domineering, a bully and he drinks.'

'Sounds all right.'

'He is, actually.' She smiled. 'You'd like him, Les. He's resentful, bears grudges.' Les sat down and began to eat his toast.

'What about him then?' he asked.

'He wouldn't mind if we borrowed his guns to shoot somebody, sort of thing he'd understand,' said Celia. 'Of course he'd never let me do it, he's a bit protective.'

'Don't look at me, I've never fired a gun.'

Celia's smile faded. 'Les,' she said sharply, 'don't be so stupid. It's not target practice that will improve matters, it's getting close, that's what you need.'

'I'd have to be nearly touching.'

'We're talking about shotguns, Les.'

'So what?'

'If you were nearly touching with a shotgun, you'd be all squelchy for your getaway.'

'You what?' Les put down his toast and looked across the table at her, screwing up his face in disgust.

'They're very powerful.' Celia spoke quietly. Les saw that her face was tight, ashen.

'You sure?' he asked. She simply stared at him.

Les finished eating his toast. He looked up at Celia from time to time and each time he did she was looking at him. Her face was pale, but he could see her softening, the harshness of her stare fading as she watched him.

'I've got to open the shop,' he said. 'Give Mick a run in the park. Should I leave you the car?'

'No, it's all right, but I'll have to use the phone.'

'For your dad?'

'He's in Australia.' Les started to protest. 'I'll telephone his solicitor. He'll give me the house keys. The house isn't far from here, actually.'

'You never said.'

'Well, I don't live there.'

When Les was on the path, going towards the front gate, Celia took him by the arm.

'Are you really going to do it, Les?'

'Oh yes.'

'Just like that?'

'I suppose so,' he said. 'Think about Charlie. Think about going to Charlie's funeral. It's got a nice ring to it, hasn't it?'

That evening they took Mick to the pub. They sat at the bar, close together, arm in arm.

'I went to Scotland with him,' Les said suddenly. 'You know, they've got this big house in Argyll. He took me up there. He wanted to show me, I reckon.'

'Come and stay,' Charlie had told him.

'You sure?' Les had looked dubiously at him.

'You'd like it. We could sail.'

'Could we?'

'Good stuff; down the loch, then back, goose-winged, in front of the wind. Nothing complicated.'

Les looked down at the bar. 'You met his mother?' he asked Celia.

'No,' she said softly, watching him, trying to push him on.

'Couldn't believe it. Like Evelyn Waugh. This fucking brittle, cartoon woman doing whatever she wanted. No problem. Poor old Charlie doing it back to her.'

'What the fuck am I here for then?' Les had asked him. Charlie didn't answer. He rolled his shirt sleeves down.

'Midges,' he had told Les. It was almost dark. The tide was out and the long, shingle drag down to the distant arc of water was fading away in the twilight. The hills of the loch side threw blackness back into the sky. 'Come down to the pub.'

'Pub was okay,' Les told Celia, 'you could see they liked him.' He stopped and looked at her. His face grew heavier, felt the tears. Then he made himself speak, telling a story, the words terse, thrown out at Celia. 'You know, stupid things. We were in a round straight away, wanted him to play darts. Stupid things, you know, mucky jokes, arranging to go fishing, all that. When we walked back to the house he started going on about his mother. He wasn't angry or anything, but he gave her a good going over. We sat on this jetty where there were some yachts moored. Just two or three. Pitch black it was. Told me about his mother. His dad didn't even figure. Just laughed when I asked about him. Complete fucking indifference to him, to Charlie, I mean, his parents. He went on a lot about school holidays. You know, on his own while they went off

185

somewhere. Christ, he went on and on about that.'

'Wanted to show you, Les,' said Charles. Les took Charles's hand and they sat there, quietly, in the dark.

'We sat and held hands,' Les told Celia. 'Never known anything like it.' He smiled, reminding himself of his grandmother. 'Never known anything like it,' he said again, mocking himself. Celia looked up at him, big-eyed.

'Hold hands, Les,' she said, picked his hand from the bar and laced her fingers into his.

Deborah sat in the train and watched the fields and towns flick by. Her father would be waiting for her at Winchester.

Barney had taken her to the station in York. Once her trunk and suitcase were on the train she had gone back down on to the platform and kissed him.

'What about Les?' Barney had said, his face heavy, mouth in a down-turning pout.

'You don't understand, Barney. It's not at all "what about Les". Les is fine. I'm off to Italy with Les. I shall probably, well, possibly, marry Les. It's "what about Barney?", that's what we've to ask.' Barney shoved his hands in his pockets and half turned away. 'We've got to fit you in somewhere.' She smiled at him and grabbed a handful of his pullover, jerking him back towards her.

'Get on the train,' Barney had said. Then quietly, 'It'll just be the odd weekend, will it?'

'An afternoon here and there I shouldn't wonder.' And she had grinned at his expression as she grinned now, remembering it.

Susan Holland held Les's hand. 'Poor old Charlie,' she said. Les and his mother and father were sitting in the kitchen.

'Are you all right?' said Susan.

'Yeah,' said Les, 'I'm okay now.' He saw his mother's eyes big with tears and he held her hand in both of his. Les remembered his mother and Charlie the first time that Charlie was in Northampton, how she had turned him into a child.

'It's just ordinary,' Les had told him. 'You know, an old semi done up a bit.' Charles looked back at him, uncomfortably. 'Biggish,' Les went on, then fell silent. Charles took his arm, gripping the biceps tightly, smiling.

'Servants? Gardener? Cook?'

'There's my mother.'

'Sounds good.'

Les turned sharply. Then he saw Charles, his face grave.

'What's up?' Les asked him.

'Which one is it?' Charles said, brusque. Les pointed.

'Just down there a bit.' Les pictured himself and Charlie looking at the road curving in towards them. On their left were the solid semi-detached houses: pebble dash and red brick, low fences overhung with jumbled hedges of conifers and shrubs. Big, self-satisfied houses looking over the noise of the road on to heavy summer trees in the park and behind the trees a sweep of grass sloping down to the lake.

Les's mother was in the front garden. She wore a straw hat and when she looked up at them Charles saw her white skin, fine red hair pushed up out of the way for her to work. She rubbed the dry earth from her hands and hugged Les.

'This is Charlie, Mum,' he said. She shook Charles's hand and stared at him.

'Susan,' she said. 'Come on into the house, duck.' Les put

his hand on Charles's shoulder, pushing him up the path, round the back of the house to the kitchen door.

They sat at the table, drinking tea. 'Where's Mick?' Les asked his mother.

'Your dad took him to the shop.' Then, abruptly, she said to Charles, 'What do you do, then?'

'Sorry?'

'At this university. What subject do you do?'

'Philosophy,' he said, awkward.

'What though?' and she made him tell her about epistemology. 'Do you like it?' she asked him.

That evening they had gone to the pub. 'She destroyed him,' Les told his father.

'Did you not warn the poor bugger?'

'No chance. Do you want another?' Roy Holland drained the last half inch of beer in his glass and handed it to Les.

'Yes, please, you go steady though.'

The pub was crowded. Les saw his mother and Charlie at the bar and pushed his way through to them. 'How'd you get on then?' he asked.

'Rubbish,' said his mother. 'I thought he'd be good.'

'Questions were all about Coronation Street,' Charles said, sulking.

'No, they weren't,' said Susan Holland. She turned to Les. 'Date of the coronation? Gets it wrong. First cup final at Wembley? Doesn't know. What planet is Dr Spock from? Baffled. Out first round, total laughing stock.'

'She says I've got to buy drinks for her.' And Charlie was giggling.

'They're all taking the piss in there.' She pointed towards the lounge bar. ' "Oh my dear chap", they're all saying. Sounds like Tunbridge bloody Wells.'

'Burglars, was it?' said his father and brought Les back.

'That's what the police say. It seems the most likely, doesn't it?'

Roy Holland did not reply but he looked hard at Les. 'Where's Celia, then?' he said.

'At the shop.'

'Celia?' said Susan, an air of shock in her voice.

'She's good at it,' said Les. He grinned at his father. 'When they come in for some cheap earrings or one of those five-pound watches, Celia talks to them, just like the Queen, and they feel ashamed, buy a fourteen-pound watch and a nice strap, proper gold earrings that won't turn their ears green.'

Roy Holland stood up. 'Come on, Les, I'll go down with you and pick her up. We should about catch her before she has to close.'

'There's a piece of beef in the fridge, Mum,' Les said as he left his mother. She kissed him and pushed him after Roy.

As soon as Les got in the car, Roy said to him, 'What sort of a tale's this?'

'It's all right,' said Les shiftily.

'Never mind the edited bloody highlights. Start off by telling me who did it; I already know why.'

'No.'

'What do you mean, "no"? What kind of a crap answer is that?'

'Not your business.'

They drove off in silence. Roy parked the car in a concrete multi-storey near the town centre.

'Why isn't it my business?'

'Someone broke into Charlie's house, Dad.' Les burst into

tears. 'Fuck it,' he said. 'He was injured so he couldn't run away. Instead he faced them up and they killed him. If you want the details, the table, a big solid beech-wood affair, was upturned, it crushed his chest. The back of his head was bashed in as well because the kitchen had a stone slab floor.' Les spoke quickly, angrily, not looking at his father. 'Celia's here for the funeral, only there won't be one for a while, so poor bloody Charlie's lying chilled in some undertaker's drawer.'

Roy Holland put a hand on his son's shoulder. 'Les, son, there's a time when you accept things and walk away.'

Les turned to look at his father. 'Well, when I can, Dad, that's what I'll do,' he said bitterly.

They found Celia counting money in the back of the shop. She looked up at them, her left hand clutching a bundle of ten pound notes.

'Be an idea to lock the door,' remarked Les. She ignored him and kissed Roy.

'Not seen you for months,' he said.

'I broke up with Charlie, you see.'

'Yes,' said Roy awkwardly. 'Come on, let's count this lot and get off. Is there a lot?'

They ate in the kitchen. 'I'm going to stay with Celia for a week or so,' said Les, 'in the country.'

'Oh yes,' said his mother.

'Her dad's got a big house in the country.'

'Well, he only has a flat in the house now,' Celia interrupted.

'Just so I'm straight about this,' said Susan Holland, 'and it's not vulgar curiosity, where's Deborah and who's with who? Simply want to know, don't want to put my foot in it.'

She looked witheringly at Les. 'Or are you going back to your old ways?'

'Yeah, well, bloody Deborah's vanished,' said Les.

'We're just good friends,' said Celia.

CHAPTER THIRTY-ONE

'It's local stone. They're forever calling it honey-coloured but it's much paler than that and there's a sort of crust that forms on it, could be a lichen or something of the sort.' Les looked at the front of the house, not really listening to Celia. 'What do you think to it?' she asked him.

'Drive down the drive,' he said to her. 'I want to stand next to it.'

Celia drove the Fiat through the stone gateway, past the wide, curving lawns and stopped by the house's front door. Les got out and looked. 'It's big,' he said. 'Even the door's big.'

'It's open to the public at this time of the year and there is rather a large staff. Midweek, though, it shouldn't be difficult to get away on our own.'

The front of the house seemed to Les to stretch away into the distance; he walked along it a little way, trailing his hand over the rough surface of the stone. He turned back to look at Celia. 'It's all yours, is it?'

'Daddy's. Well, not even his, any more. He tried to do some sort of a deal with the National Trust, but he said in the end that they were trying to steal it from him. Got quite nasty at one time. It's all tied up with trusts now and has some sort of charity status. He might even have involved the County Council. Anyway, it was never coming my way.'

Les walked slowly back towards her through the hard sunlight made more light by the pale stonework.

'Let me show you the flat,' she said to him when he reached her. She kissed him on his mouth. He looked at her, frozen by her kiss.

'None of that,' he said and shook his hand at her as though trying to wipe her away. She grimaced. 'It's Deborah, see,' he said awkwardly.

'That's a bit grim.'

'It's not easy, being in love' – looking artificially glum now.

'And you are?' She took his arm and pulled him along with her. 'Come on, it doesn't matter, just so long as you really want to and it's hell that you can't. Where is Deborah anyway?' And then she stopped. 'Where is she?' she asked him.

'I don't know.'

'Well, let's bloody well find her,' said Celia. 'A good fuck will cheer you up no end. I know it would make me feel a lot better.'

Celia found her first go.

'Where was she?' Les wanted to know.

'At home.'

'She's only just arrived then.'

'She'll be here tomorrow. She said she'd ring us from the station when she gets there. I shouldn't think that will be before the afternoon though.'

'What did you tell her?'

'Only about Charlie.'

Les got up from the armchair and walked across the room to where French windows opened on to a stone balcony. He stood looking at the countryside falling away in a pattern of

194

fields and copses. 'Did you tell her what we had in mind?'

'No.'

'Why not?'

'She'd probably not want to know.'

'That's what I think,' said Les. Celia came up behind him and put her arms around his waist, holding herself tight against him. 'Why did we phone her then?' he asked her.

'You can't exclude people,' said Celia. 'You can't keep her out of this. Can you?' she added nastily.

After breakfast the next morning Celia took Les around the grounds.

'You don't want to see the house,' she told him. 'It's full of boring furniture. I believe that they've sat some waxwork dummies in the chairs and so on. Makes it a bit of a novelty. They could at least have made it rude; younger sons rogering the maids, that sort of thing.' They stopped at the gates. A great sweep of meadow dipped away and then rose to an horizon masked by distant trees. 'Very good for tearing around on horses.'

'You go in for all that, do you?'

'Absolutely,' said Celia. 'Ever since I was small. Daddy has always been very keen on horses; racing, not hunting.'

'Obviously.'

'Don't care for the people, you see.'

'Course not.'

'It's a serious point, you sod.'

'I can see that.'

'Racing is much more sedate.'

'Sedate?'

'The flat is, yes. Look at Degas; you can't see his horses in a muddy stampede, now, can you?' They were through the

195

gates and walking on close cropped grass. 'The problem is,' said Celia, 'keeping the sheep off the cricket square.'

'Lawks, yes.'

'All right, all right, if you're not interested, you're not, I suppose: no sex, no horses, no cricket. Bloody wonderful company you are.'

Les looked at her; her hair was flicking across her face, she wore white trousers and a ragged cotton shirt. She saw him looking at her and grinned lewdly. 'Feeble,' she said. 'Poor Deborah, rushing up here.'

'You won't be back until after one at least,' said Celia. 'So we can have lunch at, say, one-thirty and do a spot of shooting afterwards.'

Les drove off on his own to Northampton. The narrow road from the house took him past a lake where a huge swan flapped its wings threateningly as he went by. He hit the main road, then dual carriageway, finally the mess of the town. He found the station and cut abruptly across two lanes of traffic when he almost missed the entrance to the car park.

He waited for Deborah at the ticket barrier and saw her walking lopsidedly towards him, pulled over by her bag. She had her hair cut so that it was very short, almost a cap, brushed forward. Her face looked sharp, more alert. Les could feel his heart and knew he would say something stupid to her. When she saw him she smiled, kept on looking up as she fiddled for her ticket, kept on smiling at him. He took her bag from her but didn't say anything. He could feel himself grimacing stupidly.

'On your own?' she said.

'Yes.'

'I went off,' she said, 'on my own. It was a bit of a break. I'm sorry.'

'What for? Doesn't matter.'

'For Charlie, for not being around.'

'Well,' said Les, sighing, 'I've done that, the weeping and wailing.' He put her bag in the boot and waited until they were both sitting in the car before he touched her. With his fingers and then his whole hands he caressed her face, her head. She bowed her head, eyes closed, and clumsily he pulled her to him across the seats. They sat for a few moments until she pushed him away.

'Come on,' she said, 'let's get out of here.'

'You're not going to believe where we're going,' said Les, laughing.

'This?' she said when Les turned into the drive.

'And Celia,' said Les, 'very milady she is. It has an effect on her. You know, it's Daddy and the staff. Oh, and the horses, but not vulgar ones, don't you know.' He stopped himself. 'We want to have a bit of a talk with you,' abrupt, suddenly serious.

'Oh,' she said and her face fell, 'you and Celia.'

'No,' Les almost shouted. 'Not that. What am I, hey?' Deborah looked frozenly back.

'What's the drama then?'

'Come on,' he said, 'I'll get your bag.'

He took her round the house, past the small church. 'That's the church,' he said. They entered the house by a side door that led into what Celia had called the flat. 'We've got a four poster,' he told her.

'None of that,' said Celia, she was leaning in the doorway that led into the kitchen. 'Cooking,' she said, smoothing down her white apron. 'Come on,' and she turned and went into the kitchen. 'Lunch time.'

They let Deborah eat her lunch and then they told her.

'No, you're not,' she told them. 'You've having an adolescent fantasy.' Les began to protest but Celia stopped him.

'Shut up,' she said, 'shut up, Les.' And then to Deborah, 'People like us, Les and I, we don't have adolescent anything; nor have we ever. Of all the reactions you could have had, that was the worst, certainly the ugliest.'

Les and Deborah stared at her.

'You're cross,' said Les.

'Les and I are, we really are, going to commit at least one murder; we rather thought that you would have liked to join us. If you won't, you won't, I suppose.'

'I told you, didn't I?' said Les.

'Told her what?' Celia demanded, her voice clipped with indignation.

CHAPTER THIRTY-TWO

'These two goons you had with you, do they know me?' Wayne Barker rubbed his chest with the towel making the flesh, red from the hot shower, liquid for an instant. Eric Ellis looked at him disgustedly.

'No,' he said, 'they only know me.' He sat back in his armchair. 'Look, for God's sake, at the outside, the very worst, it was accidental, manslaughter. We didn't break in; we rang on the bell and he opened up to us. Then he turned nasty, he's a well-known nutter, and he starts to wave a shotgun about. We panic and there's a nasty accident.'

'What about this puff up in York, what's his name, Vernon?'

'Awkward, that,' said Ellis. 'I mean, how long had your picture been stuck under his desk?'

'Not long,' said Wayne Barker.

'How do you work that out?'

Wayne Barker sighed and explained with mocking slowness. 'If it was put there a long time ago that would have been in term time and if it was put there in term time then Charlie boy and his mate would have given it to the press in term time so that lots of their jolly super mates could have seen the unfortunate poofter carted off.'

'Anyway, so what?'

'So Charlie's mate is playing silly buggers and I don't want him playing them with me.' He sat on the edge of the desk, fat and pink, wrapped in a white towel. 'So, Eric, you are going on a long holiday abroad and then I never want to see or hear from you again. Better for both.'

Celia opened the heavy door of the cupboard. 'Here they are,' she said. Les looked at the row of guns. He breathed heavily, looked at Celia.

'They're real,' he said. He felt Deborah take his hand and turned to her. 'You think there are choices here,' he said. 'Well there aren't. Don't worry, she thinks there are choices too,' indicating Celia with a jerk of his head.

Deborah sat on one of the stone benches in front of the house. She was warm in the bright sunlight. Before she could bear to look at the pages of her book, she had to put on her sunglasses.

Celia and Les were walking away from her, cutting the bend of the drive by walking across one of the lawns. They each carried a shotgun and Celia had a shooting bag over her shoulder. She watched them go out of the gate.

Celia walked Les almost a quarter of a mile down the edge of the great sweeping meadow that the house overlooked before she stopped him and stepped into the rougher grass and wild flowers which bordered the woodland.

She began briskly. 'What you've got there is called a side by side.' She saw Les's frightened face looking up at her. 'It's one of a pair,' she went on, hectoring. 'Don't lose it. Look at all that.' She reached over and touched the gun in his hands; her fingers traced the engraving on the silver sidelock plate.

'And the carving on the stock, there, look. They could soon find the owner.'

'Just tell me how to fire it, will you,' said Les, softly.

'Watch,' said Celia. She put her bag on the ground, took out a squat box of cartridges and opened it. 'The casings for these are plastic,' she said. 'Daddy has his own but plastic ones are mass produced.' She closed the gun.

'Go on then,' said Les.

'I want something to shoot at.'

'There's no need to kill things,' said Les. Celia laughed. She moved her feet, put the gun to her shoulder and fired.

'Bloody hell, you could have said something,' Les complained.

'You ought to fire a few times to get the idea of the noise and then we can use the ear protectors. They're in the bag somewhere.' She broke the gun and the cartridge cases flew away.

'They can trace guns from that you know,' said Les. Celia looked at him blankly. 'The cartridges,' he explained.

'Well, they always eject. I don't suppose there'll be time to grub around finding them.'

'We'll have to see,' said Les. 'Anyway, they need to find a gun to match them with.' He bent down to the bag, found the square, brown box beside it and took out a cartridge. 'Come on, what do I do?'

'Leave that for a minute.' She took the cartridge from him. 'Let me show you the gun.'

She showed him how to close the gun. 'Move the stock to meet the barrels.' She showed him the safety device and how the triggers were offset. 'Never carry it loaded and always carry it broken.' She showed him how to stand and gave him a formula. 'Front foot, forward leaning, firmly.' She shouted

201

at him. 'No, firmly. If you don't hold it firmly into your shoulder, you'll hurt yourself.' When he asked about firing from the hip she shouted again, 'No, no, it'll fly out of your hands or spin you round or something.'

Then she let him fire it.

Deborah sat in front of the house trying to read. It was a book that Barney had given to her: philosophy of science. She had read the first two essays in the Lake District in the early morning while Barney lay asleep beside her. The book brought his face back to her, serious and placid as he slept, his breath an almost silent hiss.

She had been sitting there for about half an hour when she heard the bump of the shots fired by Celia and then, ten minutes later, she could hear the shooting begin again. She sat with her book in her lap, staring across the space of the lawn in the direction of the noise.

It was not long before she saw them coming back. They appeared quite suddenly, framed in the gateway, and then they were sauntering towards her. Celia sat down on the bench at her side and said, 'I'm sorry to have been so bloody to you.'

'You might have been right to be. You really did love Charles.'

'I wouldn't put it quite like that.'

'It's how we speak in the suburbs. The codes we use are not so classically sparse.'

'Don't fall out,' said Les.

'If we want to fall out, then fall out we shall,' Celia told him. She took Deborah's hand and they sat together in the sunshine.

Les picked up her gun and took it and his own into the

kitchen. He checked again that they were not loaded and left them on the table with the shooting bag. In the fridge he found cans of beer and coke. Celia and Deborah were as he had left them. He sat on the flagstones at their feet and drank his beer from the can.

'We'll have to find where this Barker is and how we can best get him,' he said.

'Find all that in the library,' said Deborah. They looked at her. 'All sorts of directories in libraries: telephones, companies, businesses, Who's Who, clubs, newspapers, all sorts. Just find a few good numbers and ring up to find if he's there, then breeze in and shoot him.'

Les sat in bed reading; he looked around the room, warm, dark, a large Victorian fireplace. He got out of bed and pulled the curtains around so that the four poster was a silent room within a room, twice insulated against the outside.

He got back under the single sheet and found his place again in the book. God help me, he thought, if Celia sees it's Hemingway. He heard Deborah come into the room.

'Les,' she said, 'what have you done?'

'I've prepared a bed of erotic delight,' he said lugubriously. She put her head through the bed curtains.

'Come here,' she said. He got out of bed, asking her what the matter was, followed her through the door on to the landing.

'What?' he said.

'Celia's crying.'

'I can't hear her.'

'Of course you can't, you ape. There's a bloody great oak door there, isn't there?' She pointed to Celia's door. 'I saw her come down the corridor from the bathroom. She was crying.'

'She's upset.'

'Brilliant.' She waited for him to speak, finally she went on, 'We can't leave her on her own.' Les started towards the door. 'God, not you, not in your underpants.'

'Well, bring her to sleep with us.' He grinned, tried to hide it, but Deborah laughed.

'Go back to bed. I'll see how she is.'

He turned to go.

'Don't get your hopes up,' she said.

'I don't know what I feel,' said Celia. 'I'd taken against him. He's not a sexual loss; I'd given up loving him. Being ditched by him and responding to that, well, there was a certain gaiety in it: drama, loss, pain. But knowing all the same that I hadn't invested much in him, not lost anything that I couldn't get back sooner or later somewhere else.' She lay on the bed with her head on Deborah's lap and wept into Deborah's nightie. She saw her tears fall and spread, wetting the light cotton and saw the flesh of Deborah's thigh as the material clung to it. She took a pinch of loose material and wiped her nose and her cheeks. 'It's not right,' she said, 'tearing him away, just like that.' And then, in a small voice, a whisper, she said, 'He was lovely.'

'That's what Les says,' said Deborah.

Les heard the door open and close. Then he could hear nothing. The curtains of the bed parted and Deborah crawled in.

'Celia's going to sleep with us,' she said.

'Oh, okay,' said Les, trying not to tremble. Deborah sat on the bed, smirking at him. 'Mockery isn't nice,' said Les, 'it can be hurtful.'

'Me?'

'Look,' said Les urgently, 'what am I supposed to do?'

'How do you mean?'

'All right then,' said Les, trying to be dismissive, 'I would have thought that there were at least some questions of etiquette, precedence even, that you might give me a bit of guidance on.'

'Precedence, what do you mean precedence?' said Deborah, her smile fading.

'Well . . .' began Les.

'You'll have what you're given' – she paused – 'and like it.'

Once he got on to the M18 the traffic thinned and the orange lights made the driving easy and fast. Wayne Barker switched on the radio and got *Book at Bedtime*, almost switched it off before he realised that it was a James Bond story. He left the radio on all the way up to York, listening to the financial news that he hardly understood and the urgent trivia of the politics.

He checked into the hotel, looked across the lobby to the bar, thought better of it and asked the man behind the desk to send sandwiches and a bottle of wine to his room. He had a shower and lay on the bed in his pyjamas. There was a knock on the door and he shouted above the noise of the television.

'You're new,' he said to the fat young woman who brought his sandwiches to him.

'No,' she said. 'I've been here ages.' She thought for a moment. 'Nearly three years.'

He looked down at his sandwiches. 'Salmon are they? Tinned?'

'No,' she said.

'What? Doesn't matter.' The girl was opening the door

when he asked, 'There was someone called Mary last time I was here?'

'That's right,' said the girl, suddenly staring at him, stiffening.

'Is she about?'

'You know her, do you?'

'Get her to bring my breakfast, will you?' he said, laughing at the girl's primness. She turned abruptly, closed the door behind her.

He was watching a film, drinking his wine, when the door opened.

Mary Wilton was a tall girl with long, crimped hair dyed jet black.

'Great stuff,' said Wayne Barker.

'Half an hour,' said Mary Wilton, trying not to scowl.

'For fifty quid?'

'Hidden hand of the market, isn't it?'

CHAPTER THIRTY-THREE

'He's in York,' said Deborah. She had watched them as they came back from shooting, walking through the gate, over the lawns, up to the house. She stood up from the stone bench as they came up to her.

'He's where?' asked Les. 'What's he doing there?'

'His office, main office in Watford, say he's in York. I told the woman I spoke to that I was working on the *Sun* and that we wanted to follow up the poofter and the picture story and she said that was why he was in York; to pick up the picture because he likes pictures so much and this one especially. Then she swallowed a couple of Valium to shut herself up.' She finished with a flourish as if she were a magician. They stared at her.

'Right then,' said Celia, her voice shaky, 'let's get on the road. We can be back for dinner.'

'Don't be silly,' said Les, whispering as the fear grew in him. 'No. Let's pack, be ready to spend a couple of days.'

'We'd better take both guns,' said Celia.

Deborah drove. Les sat in the back with Celia, holding her hand so that Deborah couldn't see.

'Get you used to the car,' said Les.

207

'I'm used to it. Drove all round town this morning.'

'What do we do in York?' asked Celia. 'Where do we stay?'

'We don't have to stay,' said Les.

'There's no rush,' said Deborah. 'The important thing is to get away, clean away.' She glanced round at them quickly. 'You're holding hands.'

'I'm scared,' said Les.

They parked the car in a side street outside the city walls, a little way beyond Micklegate. Deborah said, 'He's staying at the Manor Hotel, big place by the river.' Les looked at her in surprise. 'They tell you anything and everything, when you're the press,' she added.

They got out of the car and walked down the hill towards the station.

'I don't know what this guy looks like,' said Les.

'Well, that's fucked it,' said Celia.

Celia booked into the hotel. She bought a smart, nondescript suit in town, changed in the toilets at King's Manor and took a taxi to the hotel.

She took her own luggage to her room, let herself in and unpacked. She threw her few clothes on one of the beds, hung her jeans up in the wardrobe. The room had G-Plan furniture and Woolworths pictures; it was smart and clean and smelt new. Celia liked it. She turned on the television and watched the early evening news.

When she went downstairs the girl she had spoken to at the reception desk when she booked in was gone.

'Excuse me,' she said to the dark girl behind the desk. 'I'm trying to contact Mr Barker. He's staying here, I believe.' She

smiled at the girl and saw her eyes look anxiously past her.
'He is here, isn't he?'

'Yes,' Mary Wilton said and Celia wondered at the anxiety
in her voice.

'I'd like to contact him,' said Celia and waited. The girl
looked at her. Celia gave her a smile, wondering what was
the matter with her.

'I can't really tell you,' said Mary Wilton, 'not just like that.'
Celia made her face fall.

'Oh,' she said glumly.

'I could give him your number.'

'I'm staying here,' said Celia, 'in the hotel. Can't you ring
him now?' She saw the girl hesitate. 'Go on, I'll wait in the
bar.' The girl picked up the telephone and Celia turned to go.

'Oh, stay there, it's ridiculous.' She dialled the number.
'Who are you anyway?'

'Maureen Bailley,' said Celia. 'University newspaper,' she
added as Mary Wilton started speaking into the telephone.

'Yes,' she said, 'she's here now,' and handed the phone to
Celia. She reached over and covered the mouthpiece with her
hand. 'You want to be careful with him,' she said softly.

'There's nothing to it,' said Les. 'We've got to have a phone
number that's all. Out of term there's only Barney.'

'He hardly sounded welcoming, though, did he?'

'Deborah.' Les stopped in the middle of the pavement,
poked his face forward into hers. 'He never does.' She took
him by the arm and pulled him along into a walk again.

'Well, come on then.' She was more frightened now, of
Barney, than when she had sat listening to the guns being
fired in the woods. It was last night, she thought, making love
to Les and Celia; she felt too exposed now to tough it out in

front of Barney. If Barney betrayed her, she would be lost; she felt the despair ready to crumple her. They were walking quickly. They were out of the shopping streets, past the walls, almost in Barney's street. They turned the corner. The houses had narrow front gardens almost wholly taken up by bushy privet hedges. Trees seemed to grow directly through the paving slabs.

'You okay?' she asked him. Les shook his head.

'No,' he said. 'I feel terrible, I feel sick.' He looked at her and again they stopped walking. 'I sent him the picture when I should have given it up.'

'It's not that,' said Deborah.

'No? That's what gets me.'

'What about Celia?' They stood looking at each other on the empty street and Deborah felt her blood drain so that she lurched forward, had to steady herself against Les. 'Do you want Celia?' She spoke as rapidly as the thought came to her.

'You gave her to me,' said Les and the words made him feel foolish. Then, 'Yes,' he said, 'yes, I do.' He put his arm around Deborah's shoulders, drawing her into his side so that they walked awkwardly. He pushed her first through Barney's gate. She stood in front of him at the door and he reached over her to ring the bell.

'Don't be mad, Barney,' said Les. Barney looked at Deborah, panicking at first, then over to Les. Les was looking away from him, said softly, 'Barney, let us in.' Then, almost mumbling, 'Charlie, he's been killed, Barney.'

Bernard Guy let them in and told them to go and sit on the settee. They sat side by side, like children, holding hands. Barney sat facing them and Les told him the story about burglars and an accident and Barney knew that he was being lied to. He offered them tea and chocolate biscuits, didn't comment.

'Don't say a word, Barney,' Deborah whispered when she followed him into the kitchen. 'It's too much, all this.'

'What do you want me to do, Les?' said Barney. Les looked at him, seemingly puzzled for an instant.

'We just need your phone, Barney, clear a few things up, you know. We gave your number, it was the only one we had in York. There's nobody about now.'

'To pass on messages?'

'No. Can we wait?'

'It's this fucking picture,' said Barney, softly.

'No,' Les shook his head. 'No, it's not. It's Charlie's bits and pieces.'

'Student journalism is much more professional now,' said Celia, putting a bright edge into her voice against the noise of the crowded hotel bar. 'It's important for someone like me to be in there when the national prizes are awarded. The first five years of anyone's career are obviously crucial. Getting mentioned in the prizegivings is as good as a job offer. There's real money invested now in the production side of university newspapers and magazines.' She leaned across the table and made a little upward gesture of her hands. 'In fact, anyone like you, investing in higher education, should get into the journalism, the broadcasting. That's where the growth and the energy is, not the arty nonsense, too sedate all that, one set of parasites after another looking for handouts.'

Wayne Barker smiled at her and sipped his gin. 'All right, all right,' he said, smiling, 'what do you want?'

'The details,' said Celia, 'what was said about the theft. The university's dealings with the police, did old Frank Vernon do it? Who said what? We know the story well enough, we want some texture now. What did you say to the V.C. for example? Did he crap himself and so on? I'd like to tape the interview with you, write a draft, come back and discuss it.'

He sat back and looked at Celia, leaned forward, whispered, 'Do you fuck?'

Celia managed a smile.

Bernard Guy answered the phone.

'Barney?' said Celia.

'Yes.'

'Hello, Barney,' said Celia. She tried to be bright. 'Have you got Deborah there and Les?'

'That's right.' He stopped speaking and waited for her but her silence forced him to ask, 'Are you coming round here? Stay if you like.'

'No, I don't think that we can. May I speak to Les?'

'Celia, I'm sorry, about Charlie.'

'Shut up, Barney. You're a nice man, but just right now, shut up, will you.'

'Right. I'll get you Les.'

Les was standing at his side. He took the phone from him, said, 'Yes,' and stood listening. He put the phone down. 'Did you hear that?' he asked Barney.

'You cheeky bastard.'

'Sorry,' said Les. 'It wasn't meant nastily.' Les took a big breath and when he let it out, he shuddered.

'What are you doing, Les?' said Barney softly and he put his arm round Les.

'Got to go, Barney, son.' Les was almost whispering. He grimaced and then called through the open doorway to the lounge. 'Deborah, we're off.'

212

'What are you doing?' said Barney. 'You look terrible, both of you.'

'How do you know?' said Deborah.

Les managed a grin. 'You've not seen us,' he said.

They sat watching the slick, shiny water of the River Ouse slide past them in the lamplight, the wind frantic above them in the dark trees.

'There's no way,' said Les. 'Put it out of your mind.' He was sitting sideways on the park bench so that he looked sideways across Deborah at Celia. 'Dirty bastard.'

Deborah leaned back and stretched out her legs. 'Got to get him out of the hotel.' She looked at Les's pinched face. 'This is no time for a tantrum, Les.'

'The dirty, sordid bastard,' said Les. The girls said nothing and he saw their two faces, hard and white, staring over the dirty water.

'Pub? Dinner? Party? What do you think will bring him out?' asked Deborah, looking straight ahead.

'All of them,' said Celia, 'big night out.' She spoke quietly so that Deborah felt for her hand.

Deborah said, 'Phone him and arrange to meet him. Make it a car park.'

'A lay-by,' said Les, 'Tadcaster Road, past the Knavesmire. Do you know the one I mean?'

Celia shook her head but Les could see himself there, see himself doing it.

CHAPTER THIRTY-FOUR

Les drove south again. They found a hotel near Selby, an old building with uneven floors. The rooms were rich with dark, polished wood, their bedroom like an Edwardian drawing room. They sat drinking tea, Deborah in an armchair, Les on the bed.

'Why are you doing this?' Les asked her. 'You didn't believe in it. I mean, it's no small thing, is it?'

'I'm doing it a bit at a time. You know, breaking it down, plodding through and not thinking.'

'No, you're not, it's not like that.' They sat in the still room not knowing what to do with each other.

'I couldn't say no. Couldn't face it.'

Les sat there looking at her, feeling the burden of her for the first time.

She bowed her head. 'I was with Barney, when you couldn't find me, when term finished. We went to the Lake District for the weekend.'

'Shut up.'

'So, I couldn't say no to you when you were so . . . as if you'd lost a lover.'

'I wish he had been.'

215

The next night they sat waiting in the car in the lay-by, the open black space of the Knavesmire spreading out to their right. Les sat in the back of the car; Deborah was in the driver's seat. She had slid down so that her head was almost below the level of the steering wheel.

'What's the time now?' said Les.

'Two minutes after ten.'

'Think he'll come?' She didn't answer. 'Deborah?'

'Yes, he'll come. Celia says he sounded slobbering keen.'

It was dark in the car, but Les thought that it looked like daylight outside in the street lamps. 'Start the engine,' he said.

'It's started,' Deborah whispered.

One of the shotguns was on the seat beside him, loaded and closed, with the safety on.

Celia was outside the car half sitting on the bonnet. She had on jeans and a dark tee-shirt. She watched the cars coming towards her out of York. There wasn't much traffic. An occasional set of lights lit her up briefly. Then she was held in a sweep of light which steadied and held her.

Les opened the door, just eased it off the lock. His heart pounding up into his throat. He held the door with his left hand, had the gun in his right. Celia stood up from the car and walked forward. Wayne Barker sat in his car and watched her, held in his lights.

'Lights,' Celia called to him, waving her hand in front of her eyes, half turning from the glare. The lights went off. At the side window she could see that it was him. As she moved away Deborah turned on the headlights of Les's car. Celia saw Wayne Barker cover his eyes, his big, white face suddenly there.

In the glare she was blind to Les coming out of the car. He

held the gun up, vertically, pushed over the safety lever. As he walked the six paces through the light, almost up to the bonnet of Wayne Barker's car he felt himself slowing, was slow bringing the gun into his shoulder. Then felt it cold against his face and he clutched it fiercely into himself and shot Wayne Barker, through the windscreen, with both barrels.

Deborah pulled out of the lay-by and drove towards the town. She drove them through Micklegate and into the town centre. Celia sat in front with her. Les was in the back with the gun under his feet. She came out of the city again, through Fulford and along the dark road to Selby and the anonymity of the M1 and the south.

The lights in Selby frightened Les and he shrank down in his seat away from the faces on the street. The motorway calmed him.

'Don't go fast,' he said.

'He speaks,' said Deborah. She glanced across at Celia, 'What about you? Speak, you silly bitch.' She spoke softly, gave Celia a little push.

'Well then,' said Celia. 'I was just thinking . . .'

'What?'

'It's okay now, we can forget it.'

Les listened to them talking and fell asleep. When they woke him he could see Celia's vast white house, towering, ready to fall on him.

A selection of quality fiction from Headline

All Headline books are available at your local bookshop or newsagent, or can be ordered direct from the publisher. Just tick the titles you want and fill in the form below. Prices and availability subject to change without notice.

Headline Book Publishing, Cash Sales Department, Bookpoint, 39 Milton Park, Abingdon, OXON, OX14 4TD, UK. If you have a credit card you may order by telephone – 01235 400400.

Please enclose a cheque or postal order made payable to Bookpoint Ltd to the value of the cover price and allow the following for postage and packing:

UK & BFPO: £1.00 for the first book, 50p for the second book and 30p for each additional book ordered up to a maximum charge of £3.00.
OVERSEAS & EIRE: £2.00 for the first book, £1.00 for the second book and 50p for each additional book.

Name ....

Address ....

....

....

If you would prefer to pay by credit card, please complete:
Please debit my Visa/Access/Diner's Card/American Express (delete as applicable) card no:

Signature .... Expiry Date ....